# BREAKING & BLEEDING OF A MACHO MAN

## PHOBIA OF LIFE

### BY ISABEL DELIA GONZALEZ

Sketches by Alexa Dendy

**WPR BOOKS: Helping Hands**
624 Hillcrest Ln, Fallbrook, CA 92028
760-579-1696   kirk@whisler.com

# Breaking & Bleeding of a Macho Man
# Table of Contents

# Acknowledgements

**Special thanks to:**
Stella Gilbert

Carol Huffman

Mary Huff

Katharine A. Díaz

Sketches by Alexa Dendy

Thank you Homero Gonzalez for

providing the cover photo

**Back cover & other photographs are from:**
Robin Lea Collins, President & Founder
**Heritage Discovery Center/RANCHO Del SUEÑO**
Equine division of HDC
40222 Millstream Lane
Madera, California 93636, USA
www.ranchodelsueno.com
hdcincrlc@aol.com

# DEDICATIONS

To David, the constant enthusiast

To my mama and papa who continue to love me

To Judith Campbell, M. D. – Bearer of Truths

To my Courageous sister Nelly

To el compadre Rudolph Abundis making it possible for Mexican families to pursue the American Dream

Pride comes before disaster,
arrogance before a fall.

Proverbs 16:18 (CEB)

The object in life is not to be
on the side of the majority,

but to escape finding oneself
in the ranks of the insane.

Marcus Aurelius Antoninus Augustus
121 AD – 180 AD

# INTRODUCTION

## THEIR LAST WALK

Her father made it clear he didn't want her to interrupt him. He wanted to speak in English. He did not have to be apologetic. As his daughter she was fulfilled in knowing, he no longer defined himself by others. Whatever language, the imperfections did not matter. He would start and stop and in his way of speaking he may turn in circles. Nonetheless she would understand him. Having a lifetime of hearing him practice his English he finally found his confidence.

They walked arm in arm and she wondered if she had the stamina to walk under all the umbrella trees which appeared to fall off into the horizon.

Her father began his story.


Sincerely,

Isabel Delia Gonzalez

*Family Trees*

## 1. Israel Guerra and Isabel Guerra [Benavides]

*Ricardo Guerra*

- **Angelita Guerra [Cadena]** — 27
- **Romulo Guerra** — 26
  - **Maria Benavides [Guerra]** — 21
- **Francisca Benavides [De Los Santos]** — 25
- **Fernando Benavides** — 24
  - **Juan Benavides** — 20
    - **Isabel Guerra [Benavides]** — 9 — *2...*
      - **Israel Guerra** — 7
      - **Ricardo Guerra** — 2
      - **Gertrudis Flores [Guerra]** — 5
- **Josepha Guerra (adopted) [Garza (adopted)]** — 19
  - **Israel Guerra** — 8
    - **Alfonso Guerra** — 4
    - **Ignacio Guerra** — 3
- **Angelita Guerra [Cadena]** — 23
- **Andres Guerra (adopted)** — 18
- **Romulo Guerra** — 22

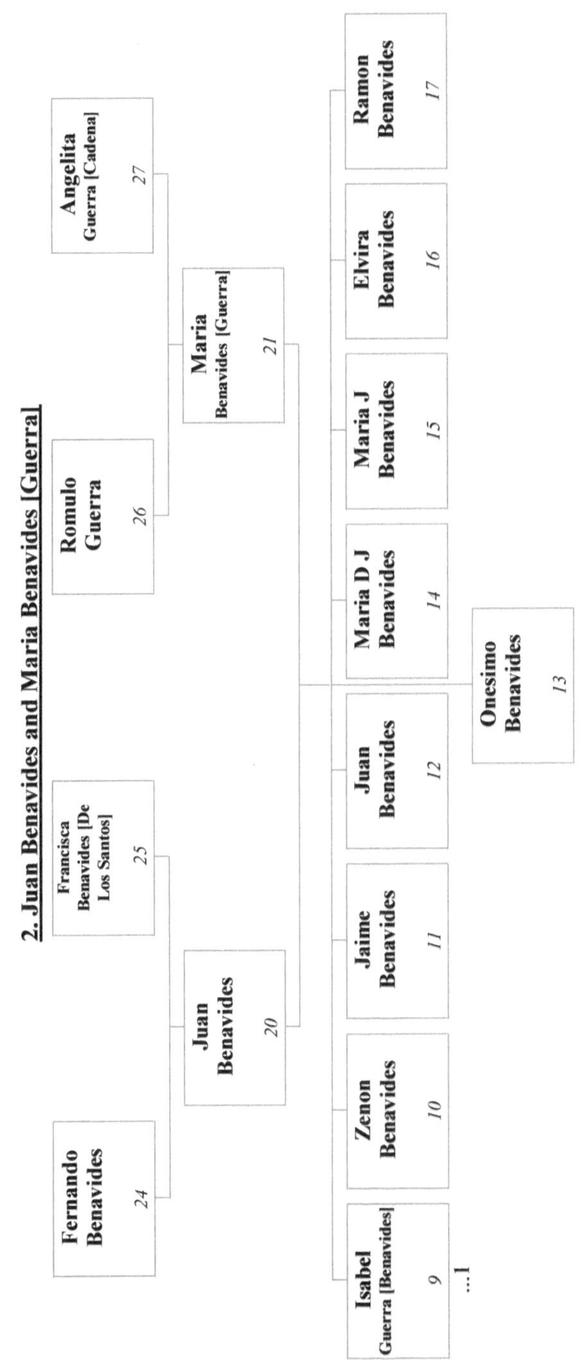

2. Juan Benavides and Maria Benavides [Guerra]
Fernando Benavides
24
Francisca Benavides [De Los Santos]
25
Romulo Guerra
26
Angelita Guerra [Cadena]
27
Juan Benavides
20
Maria Benavides [Guerra]
21
Isabel Guerra [Benavides]
9
...1
Zenon Benavides
10
Jaime Benavides
11
Juan Benavides
12
Onesimo Benavides
13
Maria D J Benavides
14
Maria J Benavides
15
Elvira Benavides
16
Ramon Benavides
17

10

## CHAPTER 1

# "RICARDO, MY SON, OUT BEYOND THE HORIZON IS YOUR WORLD!"
# I HAD TO BELIEVE HER
# MY BIRTH WAS UNDER THE STARS

I was born on a cold night on January 20, 1928, as my mother lay on the ground under a lean-to looking up at the stars.  She suffered no pain when I went from her womb to a world where I would find the others who had come before me. My daughter, your *abuela* [grandmother] was named Isabel, but others who loved her called her Chabelita.  She and the midwife had gone to her father's farm to have me, but she found there would be no privacy in the shack. My mother did not want me to start my life with chaos, so clinging to the earth, she provided me with a tranquil beginning.   She had so much will, with high spirits like a wild mare that only my father, Israel, could break.

The midwife, Gregoria, had already delivered two sons, Ignacio and Alfonso, and a daughter Gertrudis who were all greeted by the light of a candle. When all the proper things were done with me, the midwife held me up to the dark sky in her outstretched hands. "I would be the only one," my mother would say, "was born under the stars."

My father knew before he lay down with my mother for the first time she would have his strong sons. How could my father know this about my mother? My father knew so many things about my mother, about women; I am not sure where he learned so many things. He rarely spoke about how he fell in love with her. Did he love her or did he have the desire of wanting her spirit? I would ask myself many times. Yes, the men in the town and the surrounding farms had heard of her beauty and the country love ballads she sung while she worked in the fields or when she butchered an animal. But it was my father who was impressed with her as she worked side by side with him in the sugarcane fields on her father's farm. He told her everyone knew she was beautiful. He knew it would be an advantage to have such a woman. He complimented her strength while reminding her she was also weak, like most women.

You see my daughter, my mother and father's families were happy about such a union because their two houses were tied by history. Your abuela's mother, Maria Guerra, and your abuelo's [grandfather's] father, Andres Guerra were sister and brother. Their families were the houses of Guerra and Benavides. My abuelo Andres had been adopted, so the houses were tied by name, but not by blood. The force of my father's and mother's blood runs through my very being, as it runs through yours, my daughter. There is no choice. This force of the mixing of the blood is as old as the beginning of man.

My earliest memory of my mother was when she put a strange thought into my head. She would whisper in my ear that I was more than a farmer. What else could I be? I would ask her. "A man is born with a free will," she would quietly tell me. "Your father will try to seduce you into believing the land is inside you. Your father will wrap his arms around you, pulling you back from crossing the threshold to the vast land that surrounds the old fence. He will tell all his sons that beyond the fence there are people possessed by evil. He will try to confuse you and tell you only the Guerras and Benavides can come into the land. The others would only bring their jealousy and covet what is rightly ours."

Gertrudis, my sister, could not expect land from my father because it was understood she had three brothers who, at least in her eyes, appeared more important. My father could change his mind. He had the right to do so. It was his land to bestow, to give of his choosing. Gertrudis had a valuable quality, but it would disappear; it was beauty. I wanted to believe more than anything that what was inside a human was more important than what you could see with your eyes. I believe the blind have a sense of these things that can bring them everlasting happiness.

When I was a child, I would sometimes get lost and did not know how to step into my dreams; I knew the ghosts of the Indios [Indians] walked around the shack. We were to believe they could suck the breath out of us, and we would die, rightly so, since the land we slept upon had been taken from them. In my childish ways I wanted to reason with the ghosts. How do you talk to ghosts, I asked myself?  Return to your burial grounds and find solace, I wanted to command. Leave the innocent children alone. The mother earth loved the children more than anyone or anything. "Many Indios died from the invisible spread of bad air, the smallpox," my mother would say.  My mother was of the real world I could see, but she also felt the presence of those who had died before her. She was interwoven, intricately, with the blood they had spilled on her father's land.  "The Indios would have their revenge," she would mumble under her breath. It frightened her.

My first year was my happiest. I suckled from my mother's breast. I felt her warm embrace and slept beside her and my father. For my remaining days I will remember the scent of my mother as I slept beside her; it would carry me when I was lonely.  I will always remember her being a simple woman with that spirit of a wild mare. Of course, that was before my father pillaged her mind.

Soon I was two, and my father would say to my mother it was time to send me to live with abuelo Juan and abuela Maria Benavides. Mother was now ready to take her place working beside him. She was not abandoning me. The stars were speaking to them, he would say. There was a household of women, of her family, who could nurture me. "Look at your other two sons and daughter. They are perfectly healthy; they had been sent away." It was his manner to which my mother would grow accustomed.

My mother was now released to return to what consumed my father, the addiction to what my father believed to be the purpose of his life: the farm.  Only her hands digging alongside him in the dirt could release him from his compulsiveness.

## Sent to Live with abuelo Juan and abuela Maria

When I was sent to live with my mother's parents, abuelo Juan and abuela Maria Benavides Guerra, this was the beginning of my realization that there was a world beyond my father's farm. It is important to observe where one gate closes and another one opens. My abuelo owned a farm of vast lands where he grew sugarcane, cotton, pinto beans, corn, and fruits and vegetables having names in which I had no interest. The abundance was possible, I learned, because of the crooked wide creek that made the land dark and fertile. Of course, Abuelo Juan spoke to the land, giving it encouragement, acknowledging man cannot fight nature. They both depended on the rain.

My abuelo Juan had inherited the land from his father, as his father had before him, and someday he would pass it on to his own children, he said to me.  He would tell me all his daughters would marry and hopefully to someone like my father Don Israel Guerra. The men who had futures were the ones who had titles to the land and access to God's water and who had many children. Of course he was virile; his family had grown to nine children, and if Abuela Maria died, he could always take another wife and add more children to his new branch.

Abuelo Juan and abuela Maria, their children, and their grandchildren, my cousins, never spoke about money. My abuelo did speak about the corrupt government, where an ordinary man without title to his land could only shed tears but not for too long. A man had to sustain his family. The dead spirits continuously reminded Abuelo that without the document that gave him title to his land he would no longer be harmonious with all the ones before him, those buried in the graveyard. Disputes were for the living; the dead had already paid their bribes and their debts.

By appearance my grandparents were not any better off than most of the people who followed the trails in the vast countryside or in town. Sometimes I visited away from the farm, if my grandfather needed to tend to his private affairs, taking me with him. My abuela Maria would tell him not to take me into the cantina, where she knew abuelo would buy drinks for all those who respected him, whom he wanted to believe was everyone. That was not exactly true however. Abuelo would be found clearing his throat when he saw the envious eyes staring at him. They were trying to choke him, he would say.

The townspeople would tell one another everything that was planted on abuelo Juan's land was blessed by the Virgin. My abuelo Juan would instead say, "Los premios del trabajo justo son honra, provecho, y gusto" [rewards are for honest labor are honor, good health, and joy]. "The Virgin was too busy helping someone who could not reap a single kernel of corn," he told me. He would not say this in front of my abuela Maria.  Like your mother, your abuela Maria gave daily prayers to the Virgin in front of her small altar. If a prayer to make her life better came to life, I never did see it with my naked eye. I did not know how to pray to our Virgin, but as I kneeled alongside abuela, I would blurt out the words "ayuda, mostra el camino, proteger" [help, show me the way, and protect]. I repeated what I heard from Abuela as her dark eyes were fixed on the Virgin's statuette.

My life was better with abuelo Juan and his stories of battles. He spoke of the expulsion of the Spaniards and the taking away of the lands from the Catholic Church.  It was quite an intriguing conversation compared to those of my father, who spoke about animals needing to be butchered, pigs needing to be purchased, and the bull having his way with a stranger's cow and being paid handsomely. My father liked to remind us, and anyone else, that he had no tolerance for good efforts. Or he would tell us that, "Garanon que no relincha, que lo capen" [the stallion that does not neigh should be castrated]. Get rid of the worker who does not perform. It is not to say my father did not have pity. If an animal became lame, he put it out of its misery quickly. He did not want an animal or human to die slowly. He did not speak of past glories when he took the trails to Oregon.  It was a means to an end; there were no daydreams of Oregon to speak of. There were no battles to speak of. My father, Don Israel Guerra, could not know how to frame an epic story because man had only one purpose, producing something for the sole purpose of being consumed by man. How could abuelo Juan be so outreaching into the stars and Don Guerra so planted solidly onto the ground?

Within my own life I always believed there were more adventures than follies. Was it not better to think, when the mind and body are weak, there was a waterfall cascading over a cliff from the highest point in the heavens? My father could not believe of a waterfall cascading over a cliff in the highest point of the heavens. Being so one dimensional, he might as well have been a stick man.

# CHAPTER 2

# THE LAUGHING TIME

The pupils of abuelo Juan's blue eyes dilated and saliva dripped from the corners of his mouth as the memories intoxicated him. Looking into those eyes, I would try to find his God. "Only God could save the Spanish blood so there was not a total dilution from the inevitable mixing," he would say. And he could only hope his children would tell their children the memories about their ancestors' long voyage across the ocean, the long walk from Veracruz to the glories in Monterrey, to Cerralvo, and then the colonization of their final home, a Spanish settlement. God had given him, through his father, the tall stature from a line of Spanish noblemen, but his weakness of an alcohol-loving palate had, of course, come from his mother who was weak like all women, even if she had a tinge of the Spanish backbone.

Abuelo Juan's stories were of his sons and the men who had gone before him. The daughters' stories were like those of the women who had come before them. They could die during childbirth. "It could be heroic to die; after all, they could be replaced," he would say.

Another story was about his son, Ramon, who had died on the road to General Trevino. Ramon and his brother, Jaime, were traveling in search of a doctor to cure Ramon of an ailment that was not identifiable. He was despondent and could hardly breathe. The two oxen pulling the wood cart could not go fast enough, and Ramon died. While the rain was pouring, his brother had to dig his grave on the side of the road.  When Jaime returned, abuelo Juan yelled, "So, did someone put a stone on my son's grave?" Immediately one of his daughters, Maria de Jesus, Maria Josepha, or Elvira, would yell, "Sí [yes] papa, there is a rock on the grave." "I guess a rock will do," he would say. We all knew what he believed. When a person died, only a small headstone needed to be placed on top of the grave. The only people who build monuments to the dead are those who have truly neglected the dead ones while they are living.  Everyone who entered onto his land knew his son Jaime had buried Ramon without a marker.

As he pointed his finger to the side of his head, abuelo Juan would say my father was a very boring person. He lacked imagination. It was not his fault; he had no stories to share. His father, Don Andres Guerra, had no history. Too many bastard sons were left over from the revolution and from Frenchmen who were there to document the atrocities of the revolution, and that was true of my grandfather Andres. Regardless of how he could appear to be of aristocracy, he had been a throwaway child.

When evening came, abuelo Juan, barely sober, would take his place around the fire pit with my aunts, uncles, and cousins looking into the fire as it spun off red and blue sparks with black smoke rising high into the sky lit by the stars. He had to have noticed that these relatives, who had heard his crazy stories before, would only stay long enough in the circle to make their presence known. One by one they would go to the sleeping quarter, which was no more than a shack. But when abuelo spoke of it, you would have believed it was a castle. "The home built by the Benavideses would last through eternity," he would proudly say.

Abuelo Juan had depth, but his children could not see this because the words he spoke were spat out in a drunken stupor. His offspring knew this son of noble Spaniards could become a wild animal who needed to be tied down when the drink overcame him. Onesimo and Jaime would always leave last, giving a little respect to their father. They did not like his ways of spending money on tequila, but what were they going to do? Even a knowledgeable man like abuelo had his faults. A man had to have honor and respect from others. As I observed abuelo Juan, I saw how it bothered him when his sons and daughters did not show him respect. I would ask myself if his sons would learn that being too prideful or the women being too pure would not necessarily bring them respect or happiness?

Even though I heard abuelo's stories from the time I could remember, I never tired of them. abuelo Juan spoke about the Indio spirits that roamed throughout Mexico, floating above the Spaniards' graves close to the Catholic churches. These gravesites had been purchased. A giving act of charity determined who would be first to enter the kingdom of God. The Indios wanted to haunt them for all the murders, the taking of land, and the taking of Indio women for the creation of illegitimate children running throughout Mexico. "To hell with the Spaniards, look at me," Abuelo would say; "the Indios will hunt me down just because I have Spanish blood in me." He would stop shrieking and look out in the distance as if he were waiting for an Indio to fall from the sky with the intent of killing one of his children.

Abuelo Juan was tall in stature, stocky like a bull with blue eyes and blonde hair with visible white skin around his neck. The ends of his bushy mustache shot upward toward the sky, and I was allowed to touch and pull them. The most noticeable feature of abuela Maria was her long arms, disproportionate to her short stature. Her childbearing years had made her stomach swell so that her torn and faded dress rose above her knees, while the back of the dress hugged the back of her heels. She was not beautiful, but her dark eyes were soft when she spoke.

In her youth abuela Maria believed she was fortunate that such a handsome man, as my abuelo, would have an interest in her. She must have had some beauty or some strength, she told herself, because she had no money or land. Maybe he believed she could provide him healthy children, who could work alongside him in the fields.

You could only say abuela Maria was a slave. Curses and blows were an everyday occurrence. Of course, she could call herself his wife; but she was a slave nevertheless. In her life she was no longer fearful of abuelo, because she knew what to expect of him. She did not consider herself sinless, but she believed she was not a victim. She wanted to believe her children would inherit the best from both of them.  Behind those dark eyes, though, you could only wonder what she had endured living with abuelo Juan. As a young girl coming of age, abuela had heard the stories, from strangers and family alike, that abuelo Juan was the son of Don Fernando Benavides, a landowner. He was a young man in line to inherit vast lands, and the topic of his drunkenness had been pushed into the crevices of the Benavides family tree.

Now uncles would say in whispers that abuelo Juan was going too far and could no longer be trusted with the money. Who of them would stand up to abuelo? None of them! There would be an occasion when abuela Maria would scream, "You are a worthless drunk," and run somewhere, anywhere, and hope when she returned he was listless or possibly in a coma. abuela Maria would sit in the entryway of their home hoping abuelo would fall over to be picked up by his sons and be carried to the bed their father had made with his own two hands.

2

# CHAPTER 3

## "ONE WORD FREES US OF ALL THE WEIGHT AND PAINS OF LIFE: THAT WORD IS LOVE" ~ SOPHOCLES

# HIS NAMESTAKE

Another evening would come, and the firewood crackled, and the whites of his eyes turned red. One of his stories was of his son Juan. A wild cat with monstrous teeth had taken haven near the farm. The cat would devour a whole chicken in one swallow and spit out the feathers. This monstrous cat would attack children and even a man or woman. "One day," abuelo said, "my son Juan came to me with tears rolling down his eyes, determined to track down the wild cat and bring back the carcass and feed it to the buzzards. The buzzards would have such a feast, and it would make them strong."

Only fifteen years old Juan, his son, was pure of heart, and evil had not entered into him. Juan left the farm carrying only his machete and a full flask of water. Two days passed. My abuelo was not concerned, because it was not unusual when his son went on a hunt, to be away for more than two days. Still on the second night he knew his son was dead. On the third day in the afternoon a passerby, a stranger with a wagon, came up toward the fence, and there in the back of the wagon was Juan. He was facing down in the wagon, and when abuelo turned him around, his intestines were outside his body, and there was dry blood covering his corpse from his neck to the bottom of his feet. The stranger had found him when he was looking for firewood. Abuelo had to think quickly. Did this old man have a malignant spirit? Of course, he could not refuse his son, so he opened the gate. The old man said he was so sorry to bring his son in this manner, but knew abuelo would want to provide the young man a proper burial. I wanted to ask abuelo what spirit had led this stranger to bring Juan to his gate. I was afraid to ask the question.

He pulled his namesake off the wagon. Abuelo thanked the old man and told him to take as much wood from their land as he could put in his wagon.  Abuela Maria cleaned her son up, pushing as many of his intestines back into the body as she could, and they buried him wearing a suit, tie, and brand new leather shoes. He would be buried, in a pine box, without his prized worn hat on his head, where the others had also been buried, in the Catholic cemetery with the people of good standing. Onto the gravestone, which was a small rock, was only his name, birth date, and the date of his death.

Abuelo's stories of evil spirits and *mal puestos* [evil spirits] remove seemed so unbelievable, but when I was old enough to take the goats out to pasture, I could see on the other side of the fence, with my own eyes, dead animals having no apparent wounds or broken bones. Had the spirits killed them? Everyone spoke about evil spirits, even my mother. Unknown to me, she had been staying in good favor with the *brujela* [witch] woman, who would cause us untold trouble sooner or later. This woman seemed to be everywhere, but from where did she first appear? People would say she was like tumbleweed being driven about by the wind. Unfortunate would be the one who had opened the door. The *brujela* could find a need for revelations and conjure various hexes on others to satisfy someone's envy.

I wanted my abuelo's stories to be true. My mother, however, did not believe her own father. "There was not a wild cat that ate children," she said. Her brother Juan had taken the goats out to pasture, stood up on a fence, tripped, and fell down on his machete, and killed himself accidentally. This is what she believed.

"Do not believe your abuelo Juan's stories," my mother would say. "His father, Don Fernando, and his father before him told heroic stories. The story of the ship that carried their ancestors across the ocean and all the Benavides family surviving is not true. There was sickness and many died. Not a grain of truth. We will all be struck down for perpetuating lies." I was not accustomed to seeing my mother turning so red in the face.

Abuelo Juan did not want any of his sons to get ideas about leaving the farm.  The only exception was Zenon. Abuelo could not deny his eldest son, who was now at a distant private school. He had indicated early on he had no interest in land or sugarcane. Zenon's sisters and brothers did not grumble or groan. They all had their mental faculties, and each would persevere, using the skills they had accumulated from their disappointments. They believed that, by being in good standing with their father, they would inherit land, the sugar cane mill, horses, and money he had hidden throughout his property.

In time, abuelo came to believe Mentura Garza, the local hired killer, had taken his son's life, instead of the wild beast. Possibly my grandfather had shamed another man at the cantina or spoke of another's man's wife in disrespect. Everyone knew dead bodies found in unusual places were a vengeance killing. Abuelo would never approach or have the name of Mentura Garza on his lips, but as he aged he lost the ability to control what he felt in his heart. As he attained finality knowing he would die of old age, he wanted to confront Mentura Garza. It was too late. Mentura had been gunned down.

26

# Chapter 4

"That which is not good for the bee-hive cannot be good for the bees." ~ Marcus Aurelius

# El Qué Perservere Triunfa

When I was a child and later became a man, I would look around, and realize we all resembled one another. There were aunts, uncles, and cousins with a mixture of blue and dark brown eyes, and our skin varied in color from a bronze to an opaque white.  There was an understanding that everyone around the campfire worked the land. There were no better or worse among us. For miles around, everyone knew the Benavides and Guerra houses had records of good deeds. With their fertile seeds, they would perpetuate their first and last names. The uniting of the two houses brought good fortune, many would say. Does good fortune come at a price?

On those evenings when abuelo Juan was telling the stories and yelling drunken obscenities, there were no discussions about rain, or pigs, or sugarcane. I do not think the others realized, but abuelo was trying to bring laughter, even if it was at his own expense, to help them forget the hard day, when the sun beat hard and hands could not work fast enough, or hens had to be killed so the disease would not be spread.

Over those years when my father was sometimes with me on abuelo Juan's farm, my father showed respect to abuelo, but he did not like how abuelo mistreated his mother-in-law. My father would say, "El que persevere triunfa" [whoever perseveres, triumphs]. Emotionless he would say, "She came into the world with nothing, but when she dies, she will die holding onto her good spirit. That is something she needs to look forward to." She had nothing else.

There were nights around the fire with my mother's family, when the flames were flickering, and I would gaze at the stars above. I wondered if there was something to dream about that was not here on the farm. Abuelo had spoken about a beautiful city you would find walking about sixty miles to the east. There was a palace, gardens, cathedrals, women walking around in dresses made out of silk with precious gold around their necks, and men with tall hats that only the wealthy could wear. There were plazas, only the Spaniards could have imagined, which the *Indios* built. The *Indios* would learn the Spanish custom of having young men and women walk in opposite directions around the plaza in pursuit of their first love, but the *Indios* knew in time, like everything else, this too would be consumed. It was Monterrey, so refined compared with the countryside, where in the latter, things could get blurry, and you could get lost in the desert for eternity.

Things took a turn for the worse when years passed and abuelo Juan lost all his land to a snake. We were not allowed to speak his name. But one day abuela Maria said his name under her breath as she asked God to forgive him. His name was Gonzalo Gonzalez. It brought so much shame on the house of Benavides. There were various stories of what happened, but the children wanted to take the law into their own hands and kill the snake. One story told was when abuelo borrowed a large sum of money from Gonzalo and repaid with sugar cane over many years. Abuelo never asked for a receipt to prove the snake had been given crops as payment. So the day came when the government official and the snake showed up on the land and said abuelo owed money. If he could not pay, the land and all the animals would be considered payment.

Could it have turned out differently? Could the snake have worked with my grandfather? Could the snake have allowed him to pay off his debt and kept the land? Was the snake just a businessman or was it more personal? I never understood how abuelo Juan could make a blunder like that and ruin the entire inheritance. Maybe I really did not know him. Could I have been so blinded, so smitten because he showed me love?

Fortunately for his daughter Maria de Jesus and son Onesimo, the authorities took their guns away before there was more tragedy. Bloodshed over land would temper your heart for a period, but it would never bring back the land. As much as abuelo believed he was in control, his weeping could not be restrained any more than the land could be moved. Hearts were broken, and then came hopelessness. The Benavides family would banish themselves from the town's historical records. It was better to change history than to accept the ridicule. Abuelo Juan came to his senses when he no longer had the illusion he would again become a master over the house of Benavides. He was a well-respected man among the other landowners. They knew the planting of abuelo's crops on their land would be bountiful. So he again tilled the soil. He gave his fair share of the crops to the masters of the land as he had promised. He was now a sharecropper.

He could not feel regret? When he heard, those who had rented the land from the slithering snake and had modern farm machines did not produce the milk and honey the slithering snake had promised, and when wild plants appeared, after the seeds were planted into the soil, there was an outcry: someone had done something to the land. The roots of these wild plants held tight, deep into the ground. They would not die. The men with the farm machines had seen, with their very own eyes, the fields full of life when the house of Benavides was not just this bird's nest it had become. The men could only see the bitterness of the land, where abuelo Juan had shed his tears. It was ruined.

Many years later, I walked into what had been my abuelo's castle. His word was true: it was still standing. In the home he built to last for his children and their children's children, the dust had taken over. I looked at the old wooden chair set in the middle of that large room. I wanted to imagine he was still there, nodding his head to greet me, belting out the laugh that was only his to share. He was so happy to see me. I was now a man, who believed that the ghost he spoke about around the fire pit had truth. Abuelo was the now the ghost who roamed the land. What in life, he could not have happily, he now had in death.

I imagined I would find abuela Maria, so young, sitting under the lemon tree on the other side of the creek, still watching from a distance abuelo with all his restlessness. Her pain was gone.

# CHAPTER 5

# RETURN TO THE FARM

And so I was back at my parents' farm. I followed my mother about as she did her daily chores. She would sometimes carry me on her hip, and she would always sing songs of love. She taught me about the hens and the rooster, feeding the pigs slop, gardening, feeding the horses, and bringing water from the pond. My father would scold my mother for her need to have me close to her, especially carrying me at four years old. But I was scrawny, and she cared more for my emotional maturity. I could see I brought out what he yet had not yet taken from her, her true nature of loving and seeing the best in everything and everyone.

I watched her prepare our bountiful meals. For our first meal we would have eggs and corn tortillas; at our second meal in the afternoon we ate rabbit or goat, corn tortillas, and always fresh milk and coffee; and for the third meal we always had rice, beans, and chicken and always endless tortillas. We could drink all the coffee and milk we wanted. Each day she would make the midday meal for all of us and even the *peóns.* Sometimes she would walk out to wherever my father and the *peóns* were working and deliver their meals. She tended her own garden, washed all the clothes, and when you would find her in the fields alongside my father, there was a calmness about her.

I do not know where she got all her energy, her life force; whatever it was influenced her so she could move always faster and faster. She would gaze out onto the horizon as she walked and pick me up quickly. Pointing, she would say, "Out there is to be your world."I would laugh with her, knowing that moving me beyond that gate would be difficult. All the stories of the evil outside the fence were too real in my mind.

My favorite times were the moments when I sat in the corner, on the packed dirt floor, and watched her make corn tortillas, all the time insisting I would leave the farm behind someday. She knew about the other side; I could not comprehend. I would find a place where young men worked in buildings and wore suits and ties. Men and women alike used typewriters that made funny noises, and their shoes clicked when they walked.  She could visualize all this in her mind. Of course, being a smart young man, I would not speak to those women and men about the pigs or tending a garden.  She would say, "They would tell you that you needed to stay out in the fields." But we know this is not your destiny.

When she was doing the drudgery work, and moisture was rolling down from her brow, and dirt was smeared all over her face, I understood why my father had chosen her to lie with him. She had sky blue eyes, a perfect oval face, and full lips. She stood tall, looking eye to eye at her husband's brown eyes. She was muscular through her arms, chest and shoulders, and the back of the legs. Abuelo Juan reminded my father he had given up this daughter, who could work the fields as well as any man.  My father would not argue the point. My mother was his, not abuelo's anymore.


## GERTRUDIS

My father did not need to be concerned that his daughter, my sister Gertrudis, would become a spinster. Gertrudis would find, in time, the best young men from the surrounding farms, who were already starting their trek to see her beauty. My father had seen how the young men looked at Gertrudis when they stopped by to buy a pig, a chicken, or goats. My father knew Gertrudis would be an investment for any young man. Maybe she should marry an older, established man, and join two houses that had good property and livestock. It was too soon to tell what my father was looking for. As for all respectable young ladies, any interested party would first discuss with my father his honorable intentions in speaking with my sister. I felt sorry for Gertrudis. Being a young girl did not matter; she worked as hard as Ignacio and Alfonso. She followed my mother, understanding there was a chance she might have to become the woman to run the household, in case my mother died giving birth to a child, or due to some unforeseen calamity. There might be typhoid, flu, or a bite from a venomous snake. I perceived death was sometimes welcome when a woman was in terrible pain. There was pain from a wound, but the pain you could not see was just as hurtful. There would be pain for Gertrudis.

I would overhear Gertrudis and my mother speaking, during the preparation of meals about my father. "What kind of husband treats his wife like a mule?" Gertrudis would say. My mother had waited a year before she married my father because he was in Oregon cutting down trees to save money to purchase the land. He had done this for her, and she had seen his determination.

"Look at you, the lack of importance you have to him!" Gertrudis would say. "Do you not want something for yourself? Do you not think you are important?"

"Of course I am important, but not as important as your father."

"That is the problem," my sister would reply. "Women are just as important as men!" Gertrudis still being so young, hardly understood the questions she was asking our mother.

Women had to think about their children. Had marrying my father been a good decision? Gertrudis had heard that my father was my mother's first cousin. That was not true, my mother would say. Her mother, Maria, was the sister of Don Andres Guerra, who was my father's father. But Don Andres Guerra had been adopted. He had come from a union of a French intellectual and a woman from Mexico City. *Chisme averiguado jamas es acar* [gossip begun will never be done]. See with your own eyes that your abuelo Andres has no resemblance to his sister Maria or her sisters. Gertrudis was too young to understand that not all unions between a man and a woman indicate any permanence. Abandonment of a child created ambiguity, but fortunately for my abuelo Andres, he found permanence in the Guerra house.

"I now have a better life than living with your abuelo Juan," my mother would say to Gertrudis. He was a *borracho* [drunk], squandering money on liquor and treating her mother, abuela Maria, as a slave. Raising the butcher knife in the air, Mother would say that a man hitting a woman, as her father did to her mother, was beyond redemption.

"Here is my advice: learn about making a feast out of the beans or corn, which will fill a man's belly, and he will now desire the next meal. Do not worry about my working like a mule. This is the way of life. I have land; I can work to my dying days. You will see the way it is," my mother would say to Gertrudis.

And there was more. "Thousands of years have passed, and it will never change. Women have children with men. We plant corn to feed our families when everything fails, or we work the fields of others. We may be fortunate to learn to dance or get married in a church. Anything is possible," she would tell my sister.

"You will need a large family to support you when you are too old to take care of yourself. You will have to sleep by your husband's side regardless of the pain in your heart or mind. Do not be in a hurry. When the time comes for you to marry, I will tell you. Most of all, understand the sowing and the reaping of crops, for they will feed you. For now," she went on, "learn as much about animals too, as they will teach you many things about life and death."

I could only wonder if Gertrudis even knew about dancing. I had never seen either my mother or Gertrudis turn in circles. I had seen abuelo Juan go in circles though, holding onto the tequila bottle, yelling, "I am a Benavides, I am a Baez- Benavides!"

Daughter, did my mother, your abuela Isabel, put her dreams in my head so I would find my dreams comforting, only to find myself waking up to the realities of the rooster's call? I knew there was a life beyond the age-old fences. I knew also, though, that you could fill your mind with thoughts of land that would be etched so deeply you would have no room for dreams to become real. But I was a boy. I was too young to unlatch the gate and fearful of the possibility of the *mal aire* outside swallowing me. Possibly I was ignorant. But how could that be possible if the people who had great influence over my life believed these fearful things to be true?

I was not like my brothers Ignacio or Alfonso. Ignacio knew early on he would become a shepherd. He had written his life story with his feet onto the dry earth. He would travel miles, going around in circles, back and forth with the herd, as the goats ate everything in their path. He understood the difference between a cry of fear from his goats when a rattlesnake was nearby and the cry when a mother goat was nervous because her kid had moved outside the protection of the herder. Alfonso would draw onto the dried soil the outline of horses and the *hacienda* he would own someday. He could also see this mirage up in the sky on cloudy days. He wanted his own farm. He wanted rich soil and rainbows.

I would be no shepherd like Ignacio. I wanted to take a risk, to pursue an adventure. Unlike Alfonso I did not want people, animals, or crops to be my responsibility when the rains did not come.

As a child, I wanted to see my reflection in my father's eyes. All I could see was the absence of something called love when my father fixed his eyes upon me.

36

# CHAPTER 6

# REASONING

When I arrived at the age of reasoning and intuition knowing right from wrong, I could not watch an animal or human suffer because of a needless mistake. Water was the basic need for animal and human alike. If an animal lacked water, the tongue could swell and make the animal uneasy. Its need to survive could provoke our father. The animal could be whipped and be at the mercy of my father's madness. A human could see the madness in our father's eyes. Still lacking a man's life force, my mother would wake me and tell me to hurry up; she would be fixing me hot cocoa. This kindness demonstrated to me her observance of my needs and wants. She would always tell me to do exactly what my father said. And I obeyed her. If he told me to move, then I would move; if he told me to sit, I would sit. In the early days, I watched my father and learned quickly that telling Alfonso or Ignacio anything twice was a waste of exertion for our father that he would not tolerate. He did not like to use his life force needlessly.  We all learned his life force needed to be used in breaking ground, milking cows, butchering, picking the harvest, and mending fences. Most of all he fought with the wild grass. He had not learned to encourage the land like abuelo Juan.

My father had about four hundred goats, fifteen pigs, ten horses, four mules, two burro, two oxen, twenty-five cattle, a mix of cows and steers, and one bull, what seemed to be countless hens, two multicolored roosters, and all the fields to sow and reap. Among all the creatures, our bull had a vitality that could be felt even when your eyes were not upon him. Even my father showed respect and feared him. Dogs and cats had a place on the farm as long, as they did a portion of their work. It was always easy to replace a dog or a cat, but it was not so easy to replace a man. The men who worked on the farm had great respect for my father. He paid them low wages, but they were fed well every day. They would see my father and even, at times, my mother working tirelessly. "What a woman you have!" they would tell my father. It was not an insult. He acknowledged their respect. "You can only hope to find someone who shares your visions," he would reply.

As I watched, I saw my father wake up to feed the horses and mules. I knew he would be lining up the cans into which the buckets of milk would be poured. We knew he would be up by five as he would stomp into the room of the shack where my mother fixed our meals. Ignacio, Alfonso, Gertrudis, and I would be awakened by our mother not long after. Going first, my father would wash his hands, and then, one by one, we would wash our hands. By this time my mother had our first meal waiting for us.

I would venture outside the shack, directly into the radiating shimmer of the sun, walking alongside my mother as she took the blankets out to be hung on a clothesline. My mother would pretend she did not smell my urine. Mistakes happened when I slept soundly through the night. It seemed odd to me that she never gave me a proper lesson on how to control my bladder. She knew if she brought attention to it, my father would have thrown me outside to find shelter with the animals. No one spoke to me directly about my problem, other than Alfonso and Ignacio, who were always pinching their noses and laughing. How could I blame them?

During the first meal my father would divide the tedious chores among us, assigning us what he thought we each could do. At first my chores were simple, such as feeding the hens and rooster. Many times I would find myself laughing with Gertrudis when she told me the rooster had as much confidence as our father. In time I would be introduced to the stalls that needed regular cleaning so the animals would not get sick. My brothers would lead the goats to graze or bring wood for fires to cook the meals, and then they would disappear into

the fields. There was so much to learn about the farm, but I could
not believe this was my destiny. My mother did not think so either.
Working alongside her, pulling the weeds from her garden, I did not
see how she could believe her own foolishness about the world outside
the fence. As I looked at my bare feet, I could not imagine wearing
shoes that clicked when you walked or not wearing clothes that had
been worn by Ignacio or Alfonso. It was all too far beyond my reach.

## DO NOT DISPLAY PAIN

For me there were no toys, but in a waste pile I found a leather
strap that was tied to metal with a wheel on each side. I would learn to
run the wheel back and forth so I could play by myself for hours. The
animals could not be playmates, and I felt sorry for them. As I became
older, my cousins would visit occasionally, and I would play with them,
but as soon as my father noticed he would give me a task. Always, I
knew if I defied him he would scold and hit me.

So many times on the farm I would fall down and hurt myself,
like all young children do when they are growing, but I would never
cry or display pain because my father would make it worse for me. It
was so plain to me that beating a child to be a better worker or because
he or she got hurt accidentally only brought fear and pain. The truth
was neither human nor animal should be beaten. They are both noble.
I believed I could teach my father how showing appreciation to a boy
could inspire a boy to climb mountains; the noble cow would produce
more milk; the horse would have longer strides; and the mule would
take the heaviest load. They would all be willing to serve the man, if
treated well.

Even though my father did not say anything directly to me, I
would observe the way he looked at me. I knew a time would come
soon when I would take my place alongside my brothers in man's work.
There was no time to waste when there was so much to do. He would
plant in one part of the field, and in another part of the field the *peóns*
would be picking alongside Gertrudis, Ignacio, and Alfonso. My father
was a very intelligent man; he knew when to plant his crops and when
to let the wildness return.  They all wanted cloudy days, and rain would

always be welcome.

If the rains would come regularly, the cows produced about thirty liters in the morning and again at night. But in too many instances, the cows would have starved without consuming feed prepared from cactuses. Those many dry days, my father would be seen cutting the cactuses, with the *peóns* working alongside of him, for what seemed to be endless hours. The thorns would have to be burnt off the cactuses, and to me it did not seem to make any sense. It seemed so foolish. The cows would be milked only once a day during a drought. Anything we did not consume or sell was given to the pigs, dogs, and cats. My mother spoke of the lean years, when men and women left the countryside, to find a field where their hands and backs could be hired. Someone else's bountiful harvest was a blessing for all. It was a good thing for the men to find rocks that had been spit out from underneath the soil. Even the women would clear the land for the man who had title to the land. Along the roads you would find dead puppies or kittens in bags by the trees. An experienced man or woman had performed the mercy killing. The starving dog or cat could not produce milk, and the newly born would starve. The people would say, "The trees were fortunate that they were not human. They unintentionally were given orders to not move."

41

Breaking & Bleeding of a Macho Man

# CHAPTER 7

# TRANQUILITY

There were days when we would find the workers having an informal conversation with our mother. Of course, my father would not let it last too long. We would learn who were married and those who professed they could not find true love, for women were so unpredictable. My mother would smile. I wondered if my father had seen my mother as unpredictable when they first noticed one another. I would need to observe Gertrudis to see if this unpredictability would surface. After everyone finished their chores, my mother would have our third meal ready for us. As I would soon learn, everyone needed to eat quickly to give my father full attention. He would tell us what each one of us had done wrong during the long day. Gertrudis, Alfonso, Ignacio, and I could not believe our father could be in so many places at the same time. The distances he would have to walk to oversee what each one of us was doing seemed improbable. Everyone was so tired, and it was not unusual to find one of our heads slumped over on another one's shoulder, with our eyes barely open, as my father still talked. There were times my father would grab me and position me upright because I had fallen asleep on my mother's lap.

We often wished for rain. Year after year there would be days when each one of us would climb a tree searching for a dark cloud on the horizon. All of us would sleep more soundly even if the rain came into the shack. With rain, my mother could expect a stronger embrace from my father. We could feel the mood of the air change. We could step easily into the deep sleep, being calm, the thoughts of drought a distant memory. The tranquility could be interrupted if you heard one of the dogs warning the wild predators that they had wandered in the wrong direction.

# CHAPTER 8

# WHAT KIND OF MAN RAISED MY FATHER?

My mother said having all her children baptized was pleasing to God.  She wanted my godfather Uncle Emeterio Guerra, my father's brother, to share with me his modern manner of thinking. I did not know why. At the time, he seemed to my young eyes to have no ambition, and he had no interest in me. Would he be the one to give me the sign for what would be my success in the future? He certainly did show compassion when he would place his hand on my shoulder and tell me that my back was straight, and I walked with purpose. What was my purpose? I wanted to ask. Tell me my future.  Tell me what is beyond the town. Tell me why my father does not see my life outside of the fence. He had gone to Oregon; he must have told someone of his adventure, yet he was wedded to the soil now.

When my abuelo Don Andres Guerra and abuela Josefa, my father's parents, visited the farm, I wondered what kind of man raised someone like my father.  Gertrudis, Ignacio, Alfonso, and I observed a reserved man unsympathetic to the world around him. My abuelo Andres Guerra, this man who had been adopted, was a man of average height, a slim man, blue eyes and pale skin, and sandy blonde hair, not only on his head but running up and down his arms. He did not amuse me like abuelo Juan, but then abuelo Andres did not drink or hit his wife either. My abuela Josepha, unlike my abuela Maria, was taller than abuelo Andres. Abuela Josepha had olive skin, green eyes, and coal-black straight hair. She had a high confidence level that could be considered by some as pretentious. Possibly, she could have been the human who scolded my father when he tried to be a boy.

The one thing my abuelas had in common is they knew not to disrespect their husbands. I wanted to ask my abuelo Andres what it felt like to be illegitimate, but we were all told by my father it was not the circumstance that a person was born into that measured a man. The color of a man's skin did not matter to my father. What mattered was whether he was willing to work, to push himself to exhaustion, to not complain, and to endure hardships.

## BREEDING

At a very young age I understood the word breeding. It seemed like such a strong animal as a bull was having his way with a cow that was not so powerful.  Afterwards, the cow was removed from that corral, and the bull returned to the daily pleasure of eating and waiting for the next cow. Months later, a cow would have to bear down to give birth to a calf, and it did not matter if the calf was beautiful. Ugly cows can produce large amounts of milk too. To me there were no ugly cows.

I had seen how people stared at my abuelo Juan. So why are people jealous of the white ones? Young and old alike would react to his blue eyes and light skin and full head of blonde hair. Underneath their smiles, they would be grinding their teeth, jealous, but they did not know that mal *puestos* had no hold over abuelo Juan. I would ask my father; he would tell me it was a figment of my imagination.

My mother did what was expected of her. She had another child, and I could not accept it. I was overwhelmed with jealousy when I heard that Israel, my younger brother, was going to be baptized, and my father was showing affection to this new son.  It was obvious to

Ignacio, Alfonso, Gertrudis, and me there was something about the new child we could not see with our eyes. The christening gown was not special; we had all worn the same gown. The same priest baptized the baby; this priest was now older but wore the same ceremonial robe. All of us surrounded this young boy like they had all done before. I did not want to know who his godparents were. All I wanted to do was to stare at the back of the altar at this Jesus who hung up on a cross. Someone had to have put him on the cross. I guess I was afraid to ask my mother why anyone would want to nail a man to a cross. I did not want to hear the real meaning of it for us, that pain could transform a person, improving his station in life.

My father believed in God, but even being a strong man, a man of reason, he could become fearful and anxious. Did I inherit being superstitious and fearful from my surroundings that day in church, because I did not ask my mother why the man was nailed to the cross? There was a belief that once your mind was fearful unrighteousness could enter your body. The body would be receptive to spells. As we returned to the farm, conventional wisdom had been established in my mind. There were more than enough real difficulties to be concerned about than with superstitions.

# CHAPTER 9

## COURAGE TO BE JOYFUL

Working on the farm, I learned the rhythm of life. The smell of the air, the motion of the wind, the light or hard raindrops falling onto the thatched grass roof easily put me to sleep. The animals gave birth, and others perished naturally at butchering time. Mother's watermelon seeds would sprout and later be heavy with fruit to be picked.  Mother's garden could provide a bounty of spices and cures for every ailment. Always, the sun's rays beat down on the hard, dry, brown earth, and the animals walked blindly around as if sleepwalking.

With a good rain Ignacio, Alfonso, and I would run to the creek. We had to use our time wisely since it was not really ours. We were hoping to find our friend, Teresa, who would jump into the creek with her dress wrapped around her waist. The fearless four of us would drift with the unrestrained water to the place where the creek turned. The bend in the creek was always the marker, the sign for all of us to go back.

The many afternoons at the creek, as I would become more astute, I could no longer deny that the conditions I was living under were not in my best interest. My father had no problem throwing blows at me in front of people and what was worse, when no one was around. He took his disappointment at weaknesses out on me at times. There was always food on the table, a thatched roof that leaked but nonetheless could provide a spoon of precious water landing on my lips, and acres of land to get lost in when I needed comfort. I had to ask whether I should let myself go adrift.

I was human chattel. Who would miss me other than my mother? I had to think that feeding me was easy now, but releasing me would be more difficult later, because I would have his brand scorched on my flesh, making no mistake of what I was to him.

I had to reassure myself that my father had goodness in him. I told myself he had perseverance, turning all the vast number of things connected to this land into working parts, which collectively defined him as a landowner. In him there must be unseen treasures that kept him toiling on. Then, too, he was well respected in the Guerra and Benavides houses. His tenant farmers and those who were invited inside the fence respected him. So what was wrong with me? I asked myself so many times.

At the creek, the four of us rounding the bend knew we would have to get up on the banks to walk back to where it had all started. All of us would have to return to our reality. Teresa would return to her unsuspecting parents, who believed they would raise her as a princess, when she preferred to be something different. She had no interest in those ready-made dresses her doting parents bought her. Instead, she too dreamed. Alfonso and Ignacio would find her in her father's truck with her hands on the steering wheel, smiling out at the horizon. Perhaps she wanted to go to Monterrey, where it possibly did not matter if women as refined as Teresa wore pants. Ignacio and Alfonso laughed at her, and she found joy in our laughter.

Alfonso, Ignacio, and I spoke about Teresa even when we saw less of her as the years passed. The thought of her being different gave me courage. Somewhere deep inside, I knew I was not so different than Teresa. I had the courage to be joyful. I could appreciate those things around me but not be confined by my circumstances.

51

# Chapter 10

## Waiting for the Sign

I turned another year older with no celebration; it was just like any other day. That morning, I could hear under my mother's breath, her gratitude to Our Lady for keeping my body strong and our dream about my future alive. I had been inside the shack pushing the broom back and forth in an attempt to move the dust outside the door to the patio, but in reality I needed to push away the restlessness inside me. Perhaps my mother, who kept the broom moving at all times of the day, was really soothing herself with prayers. I had come to believe she had no dreams for herself. Could not everyone see she was unhappy? Maybe when I was older, I could tell her she needed to go back to the time when she liked being a girl. I knew, like me, she needed to be distracted from the rhythm that sucked energy from her.

My mother motioned for me to stand before my father. It was unusual to see my father sitting down, not standing up to tell us he was going to make men out of us. I waited to hear that I had not met his expectations. I was still scrawny even though I ate as much as my two brothers. I did not have the words to express my thoughts but disagreeing with him was futile.

Today something was very different. He said I would be attending a private school to learn my numbers, to read, and to write. "Tomorrow you will start school," he told me. "We have new *ropa* [clothes] and *huaraches* [sandals] for you. You will be living with your aunt Felicitas through the week, but there will be days when one of your brothers will pick you up at your aunt's after school to bring you to the farm in the evening, depending on how many hands are needed. You will always spend weekends with us." I was afraid to show my happiness. Later, I told myself, I can yell and jump for joy.

He told me for the land to have a future and meet our needs, to succeed against the odds, there had to be a person who had good intuition when it came to identifying unscrupulous people. I was not sure what that word unscrupulous meant, but it made sense at the time that he was speaking of people who would try to take away things that belonged to my father. His shack and all the land beneath it for miles around had been eyed by all the other landowners. He had seen them on their horses as they were looking for a breach in the fence. He could not afford for squatters to move onto his land or a cow to mistakenly lead the herd onto other people's land.

I was to be the other person reading paperwork; I would be putting every single penny down in the book and understanding how the government works with all the documents needed to keep the farm in order. You could not trust the damned government. You could not trust the large landowners either. Both of them had their own desires for this land. My father said that my mother believed I was the right son to take on the responsibility of learning to manage the books. He had to agree with my mother. He had noticed how observant I was of my surroundings. I did not just react to situations. I had a good mind. My mother did not smile, but I could see in her eyes this was the sign I had been waiting for. It was going to be different. Possibly, I would learn to unlatch the fence and never look back.

As usual, I wet myself in the evening, but I rose early the next day to clean up and put on new garments and shoes. I ate my breakfast, and as my mother handed me my hot cocoa, I only hoped that in my absence she would not forget me. Riding in the wagon with the milk in the clanking container jars in the back, sitting next to Ignacio, I could not stop smiling. He took notice of my joy and told me he was happy for me too.  Someone in the family needed to understand all the paperwork, and I was a good choice. He said he had watched me many times thinking through problems, always telling the truth and most of all bringing happiness to our mother. His words gave me confidence, and when I breathed, I felt the air coming in my nostrils and it did not matter if I was inhaling dust.

I was dropped off at Aunt Felicitas' home in town. She was the poorest of my father's sisters and brothers, having married a man whom she had believed would support her and their two children. Was it her fault that she had no future as he took the easy way to relinquish his responsibilities and found solace in mescal? In their two-room shack, she and her daughters would make paper flowers to sell at various religious festivals. They were to be admired for their industrious lives, everyone would say, perhaps trying to reassure them that a good woman could overcome anything. I would learn that we had something in common. Neither one of us liked the smell of farming.

"What is so special about you?" she asked me. I just pretended she was speaking to someone else. I was to sleep on the floor, on a burlap sack full of dried beans, in the corner of the kitchen. She raised both arms to the ceiling of the shack and announced, "Everyone in the family knows about your bladder problem so we will not discuss it again." I could not deny it. I would need to bring extra undergarments to wear each morning for the overnight stays. "Your father's generosity will give me the opportunity to light a votive on his behalf to the Virgin. It is a blessing for both of us," she would tell me often. She fixed me hot cocoa every morning when I resided with her overnight as her sister-in-law had requested. "Call me Aunt Fela," she said one day. Possibly this her way of telling me she liked me.

Now on the first day, I would see for the first time a teacher who believed we all had potential. I did not have to rely on my back, shoulders, and legs to be strong. What mattered was in my skull. Possibly, inside the skull was all that I needed. I cannot deny I wanted my father's love.

## SCHOOL AND OTHER LESSONS

I would be learning lessons from school but also from my remaining time on the farm. Attending school I had only to worry about learning my numbers, learning to read, and print words. My father was a smart man to send me to school. Possibly, he was showing me love in his own way. That was a frightful thought; because it was something he could give but also could take away just as quickly. I had the desire to learn, but I also had questions about so many things.

I found some new things about myself. I could laugh at myself and with strangers. I was surrounded by people my age and older who wanted to talk about baseball and nothing about cows and pigs. I wondered if their fathers kicked these boys. There were no visible scars. Maybe there were under their clothes. Could they have taken a blow to the head? A full head of hair could always hide bruises and swollen tissue. I started climbing trees to show how agile I could be, growing confident, the inside of me becoming visible instead of hiding away from my father, shaking with fear.

School went so quickly, and I was back on the farm full time. Nothing had really changed. I again was helping my mother and sister Gertrudis. I would go through the motion of cleaning out the goat stalls, throwing the chicken feed up in the air knowing it would come down, and pulling the weeds in my mother's garden. I really did not do much very well, but I was kept busy. The clouds of dust flooding the lungs, coating the mouth, and burning the eyes were awful but were shared by all of God's creatures, my mother would say when I complained. How could any man expect to make progress, real progress, when he felt like he was choking? I did not need to look in her direction to know she was smiling.

57

*Emiliano Zapata was a leading figure in the Mexican Revolution, the main leader of the peasant revolution in the state of Morelos, and the inspiration of the agrarian movement called Zapatismo.. Born August 8, 1879, in Mexico. Assassinated: April 10, 1919.*

# CHAPTER 11

# I CAN CREATE A STORY

One day, like many days before, I tired from filling the water jugs from the pond.  I sat down in front of a large rock. I wanted to cool my bare feet by putting them in one of the jars, which held murky, chocolate-colored water. I took a large stick I found beside me and flipped the rock over to the side. I was expecting to find scorpions, but instead, I found a one-foot hole containing two rusted pistols. Could my father have hidden these? If he hid them, it would have been for a good reason. He had a locked trunk beside him as he slept. It held his shotgun and other important possessions, including the book and pencil that noted every detail of his existence.

I picked up the two pistols with their barrels facing me and wondered if Pancho Villa or Emiliano Zapata had hidden them. There were many revolutionary heroes to speak of, but these were the great men. They chose to lose their own lives so others could pursue equal standing with the very powerful and rich. To the landless they were the heroes, but for the *patrónes* [hacienda owners] they were an insult. Who were these two men believing they could change what had remained in place for over two hundred years? Abuelo, being of Spanish descent, admired these two men for their courage. They were ready to die for their beliefs which could not be said for that Porfirio Díaz.  He opened the gates of paradise to the foreigners, and they paid pennies for the land.

Díaz seduced the Mexican people with hollow promises.

*Francisco Villa was a Mexican Revolutionary general and one of the most prominent figures of the Mexican Revolution. Born: June 5, 1878. Assassinated July 20, 1923.*

Abuelo Juan would spit on the ground and slander all the foreign families and all their unborn children, who had damaged Mexico because the *Indios* and throwaway children had built it. They might be privileged, but the true Mexican people really owned the land. In the end, who are the real title holders? Abuelo Juan could not answer his own question.

"Zapata believed it was better to die standing up than on your knees," abuelo Juan would say. How did abuelo know what Zapata believed? The heroics of all the men are written but what about the women? "The women who followed these men had nothing to lose; those are the ones who followed the rebels," abuelo Juan would say.  As the Spaniards, rebels, French, and even the Comanche in the north fought for their various ideologies, there was also the pillaging and the taking of women, leaving them with children with no last names. I did not understand why abuelo Juan had to speak so much about the bastard children. Sometimes it was like a record being played over and over again. Did he have guilt?

I wanted to believe the pistols belonged to Pancho Villa, but they could belong to any person capable of killing. Taking the pistols to my father would give him reason to believe I was not doing my chores fast enough, so I placed the pistols back into the hole and replaced the rock over them. My father believed that if you raised a pistol, you should be prepared to shoot. I decided to make up a story in my head while I did my drudgery work. This would be a story of heroics to tell my children. I could never overshadow abuelo Juan's epic stories, but someday, I would have my own adventures; I would make certain to record every detail.

History is never really buried. If history is to be of the truth, then the man telling the story cannot lie. My father did not say things behind your back. He let you know where you stood with him. He stood up for what he believed to be true even when my mother gently told him he was wrong. His truth was always real. Even if his wife and children could see the sky was blue, he saw clouds that held water heading toward the farm. It was his truth that mattered. He was no different than many men of his time.  Someone had to be strong, to feel the bitterness of a snake bite and make light, as if it were an ordinary experience.

Some days I would see my father pick up the dirt from a field after a healthy rain and rub the dirt between his hard, calloused fingers. I would see his brown eyes soften in the same way that he looked at my mother, during those private times they tried to hide from us. Maybe on those days when he looked at the horizon, he saw himself as a young shepherd boy running through the fields heading toward the creek. He had to have once had childhood dreams and to have done childish things.

63

64

# CHAPTER 12

# COULD THEY SEE MY BREAKING?

There comes a time in a life when strangers tell you freely of your pedigree. Did the blending of my mother's and father's bloodlines produce children appealing enough to draw in the unsuspecting. I remember the first time Aunt Fela took me to the market on a Saturday and people said, "Look at him. He is so handsome." It seemed incredible anyone would think I was handsome. Was being handsome a good thing? "The time will come when you will find people who will value you for being handsome. Do not worry yet!" she would say.

To have value for your outward appearance did not matter to my father. It was the muscles under the skin and the memory and lessons of calamities that counted, because if you did not learn from these, you would have to go through the physical and mental pain in a ceaseless circle. I watched my father shave the manly hair on his face, looking into the mirror; I could see what the farm had done to him. He had golden-brown skin, but there was pale, white skin only appearing when he had his shirt off. He kept his hair short, but the blonde hair was always visible even when dirt or blood had worked its way into it. His eyes were brown like caramel, and he had a strong nose, mouth, chin, and a strong upper body, which was noticeable when he washed the farm from his body. He had no resemblance to anyone in the Guerra family. Would my grandfather Andres' parents ever appear? Abuelo Juan would say, "Stray dogs rarely returned, and his brother-in-law could only hope some venereal disease had eaten the stray dogs' brain."

No one but my mother stared at my father to acknowledge God had given him a strong back. She alone could make frank remarks about him smelling like a pig or forgetting to mark down in the book the dozen pesos he had received from the neighbors for the services of the bull.  She always had the right to tell him the truth. He had given her that freedom.

My mother loved that man and never questioned him about his thoughts. There were swindlers and thieves everywhere, and most of all strangers waiting to cross his land. Shadows were around every corner. My mother had an open mind. It was not us against the world as he believed. Still, there was some truth to how he felt. It was not a sickness that ran through his veins when he was compelled to repair a fence in the middle of the night. He knew how a piece of land that was not fenced could be taken by another, a man of means or a squatter left over from the days of the revolution.

Now was not the time for my mother to look at herself in the mirror. Her skin was becoming spotty, leathery textured, white skin barely mixed with new skin growth.  Her front teeth had fallen out of her mouth, and her gums were hurting her. The furrows on her forehead were becoming deeper.

So was I handsome as the people in town said? One day I climbed onto a wooden tree stump and looked straight into the mirror. I had my father's bird beak nose and oval face with sandy blonde hair, but my eyes were blue.  I told myself my nose was like the eagle's that flew on the Mexican flag at school. It was never ridiculed. Maybe I was handsome and not ugly as I was led to believe by my father. "There was no purpose in staring into the mirror," my father said. "It would always be your own reflection, unless…" He would never finish the sentence. My aunts told me to ignore that superstition. It was about people who walked the earth who later became saints and had seen their own auras in the mirror.

Sometimes in the evening, my parents would speak about how evil had found its way to the neighbor's farm and had made all the hens sick. It was a *mal puesto*, a spell that would be countered with another spell. But who had sent it? They would speak of the evil eye, and how people who coveted what you had would make you ill and despondent.

Many times people did not even know they were draining the life out of you. It was best to keep people out of your affairs, to depend on no one but the family. I could not accept people actually believed there were *brujelos*? Was I so ignorant to believe the stories? How could I believe in those things I could not see?

Aunt Fela also spoke of the *brujela* who walked freely in town and was even found walking alone in the countryside. She did not want to even say her name. It could bring bad luck. It was better to cross to the other side of the road and walk a mile out of your way than to cross her path. "Someday you will see all the neighbors close their doors, as if to protect themselves from the fury of a windstorm, but in reality it is the *brujela* walking through the streets they want to avoid," she said. Her words caused a cold chill to run through me, in spite of not wanting to believe it.

## ANOTHER YEAR OF SCHOOL

When I returned to school, I again stayed with Aunt Fela, who was now sewing and mending clothes to barely keep a roof over the heads of herself and her children. Her husband now rarely used their modest shack as a place to dream of possessions, and I could see he had no courage to change. He decided to just merely exist. Aunt Fela did not show any bitterness or resentment toward her situation. She would take the money my father gave her, and true to her word, without him knowing it, votives were lit for him. No special prayers, just the simple prayer, "Embrace him with your love and keep him safe from self-destruction, "she would say. I was not sure what self-destruction meant. It was one of the biggest words in my vocabulary, and later I would wish I had never learned it.

I perceived very early that knowing my numbers and letters very well meant my father would allow me to open the ledger, which had numbers written up and down in columns, with words noting what type of animals, eggs, and crops he had sold and how much his profit was. He had an entire page dedicated to the bull. Commenting on the stamina of the animal was one of the few times he showed any happiness. There also was a book of expenses, but I was not responsible enough to carry that information in my head yet. "I was making progress," he would say. He also knew I remembered the lessons from working beside my mother, sister, and brothers. Some I knew like the back of my hand, and some were new. "There was nothing to gain in learning an old lesson again," he would say. As I looked up at his face, gazing at the marks on the page, it startled me to realize this man could have been more than a farmer. What else would it have been? I wondered.

My sister, Gertrudis, was now twelve years old, a daughter surrounded by men. Unlike Teresa, Gertrudis first wanted to be a princess who would find a life with someone. In her dream world, she and the prince would build a life together, with her singing and wearing fancy dresses and dancing in circles under the stars. She would say to me she had no real friends other than her aunts, those ladies whom she would see when she visited abuelo Juan and abuela Maria or at church during the holy days. Gertrudis was also now attending school, but she would be reminded by her surroundings that someday she would belong to a man, body and soul. What should a woman desire? It could not be having children, cooking, butchering, and all the drudgery work put upon her. At least not for Gertrudis! I thought.

I found myself learning more about my country than just the stories I heard from abuelo Juan. I was proud of the progress of having a teacher in a rural community. We were a farming community, a backward Spanish settlement, and not very exciting compared to our capital, Mexico City, or even Monterrey, which had new industries.

There had been revolutions, but there was hope that disagreements could be settled with the stroke of a pen and not by a pistol. Hard work was to be respected, but knowledge opened doors beyond the town. That was an ideal for our emerging country. Our Mexico was going to modernize; I would hear over and over again.

My teacher, Miss Salinas, told us in class we all had natural abilities, and I had the gift of numbers. My brain needed to be cultivated to put information in and then take information out. In time we would learn a lesson and then learn another lesson related to it. That relationship could be used repeatedly to make the world around us make more sense. Looking at Miss Salinas gave me hope that Gertrudis could become a teacher. She would belong to no one but herself.

You could not see by looking in the mirror from where all this natural intelligence of mine was coming, but it made my father happy knowing he was spending his money wisely. Was I to believe in those things I could not see? I could not even see what my brain looked like, but I was supposed to believe I was gifted. So I had a brain that was gifted, but I also knew my parents spoke of spells directed from one person to another. Perhaps my mental abilities had been orchestrated by the brujela, I sometimes wondered; but I told myself, if I cannot see my brain that bears gifts, why should not I believe like my parents in the *brujela's* powers?

## BACK TO SCHOOL

I was now attending a public school in town. I began to learn Mexico was a country and there was history about this country. There were more than farm animals and crops, in preparation for becoming the promising, suitable person to manage the accounting books for my father. Yet I was more interested in abuelo Juan's history lessons. Abuelo Juan had talked about the uprisings against the Spaniards, but he, a Spaniard by descent, was disappointed about the outcome. All the independence did was to transfer the wealth and power to the children of the Spaniards who had been born in New Spain. The Spaniards born in Spain were being given special privileges and the Spanish American creole sons born in New Spain became overcome with envy.

The poor were intoxicated with the idea that the Spaniards born in New Spain had come to their senses. Rejoicing was very short-lived. New Spain died and supposedly the new Mexico would change everything. The foolish believed the war was over. The new crowned kings knew the war would never end. There was the revolution abuelo would speak of and how many had died. All it did was to confirm the splintered ideologies. Whenever he spoke of the revolution, he would look up to the sky; he would shrug his shoulders, and be lost with his thoughts. Miss Rodriguez was always speaking of the modernization of Mexico. She did not speak of the landless or why there were too many people who lived in poverty. She did not resent the landowners or crazy Porfirio Díaz. I only doubted abuelo Juan's lessons for a few seconds. Who was I to believe, Miss Rodriguez or abuelo Juan?

I tried to understand why individuals rarely spoke about their lack of money. It was obvious who in town owned businesses and who had the biggest truck – which was Teresa's father – but everyone basically dressed the same, and even the outside of the homes were all painted similar colors. People, who lived in the haciendas, had clothes made of finer fabrics, and their hats seemed to have been purchased for just one occasion, but everyone concealed their true significance. There was one exception.  Abuelo Juan refused to put the name on his lips. A woman he had loved when he was a young man, at the prime of his youth, married a man of immense wealth. The man would intentionally have abuelo's lost love by his side, going round and round the plaza, with his finest horse pulling the opulent buggy. Abuelo's eyes would well up with tears.

Abuelo Juan did say that his father would speak of the time when the church measured a man by his contribution to the Catholic Church. I said to abuelo Juan, "Hopefully, they are all with God in heaven."Abuelo would answer, "I doubt it." He did not give me lessons about God, Jesus, or the famous lady. He believed that all men were sinners.

Some thought grabbing me, an intrusive thought of geography. All the students had had the special privilege of touching the round globe setting on the teacher's desk.  Spain was so far away. How could Spaniards travel across the ocean and survive? Why would they bother establishing our backward Spanish settlement in the godforsaken land where water was so scarce? Is this where the first sin began: to covet the water?

71

Breaking & Bleeding of a Macho Man

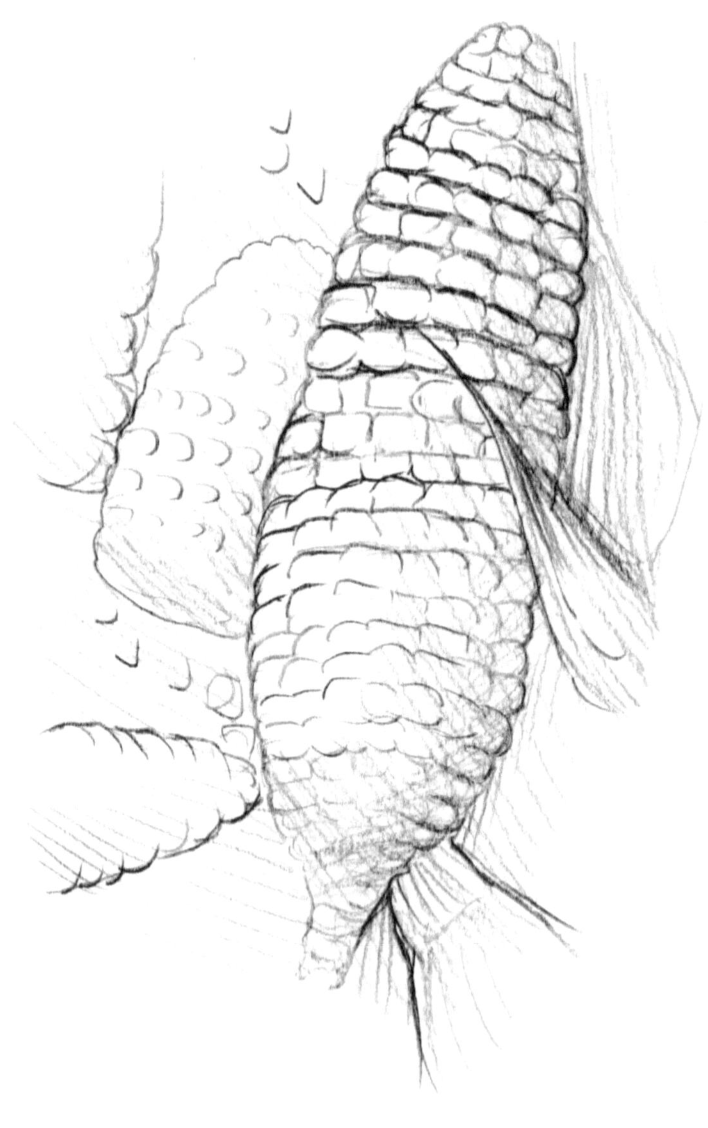

# CHAPTER 13

# THE PERFECT TREE LIMB

I cannot remember how old I was, but I remember I found myself running to keep up with my father's long strides as we walked to the fields. He would lead with the plow and the horse he called Tonta. My father believed Tonta was stupid, but I knew she would have died in the middle of the field many years earlier if it had not been for her immense common sense. She followed his commands, never going too fast or too slow. Sometimes she would prance and do what appeared to be a dance. This natural ability must have happened in her breeding so many years ago. My father would find himself in a trance, and when Tonta finally stopped, he would find himself at the end of a row.

The previous day the dark clouds had opened and brought a torrent of rain to the fields. My mother told my father in the early morning hours that the mothers in the countryside and town had prayed genuinely, more convincingly than before. The Virgin and all the angels were on our side. It was less likely now they would see themselves or their neighbors, heading north to Matamoros to the cotton and tomato fields where picking was plentiful as they sometimes had to do. "Men, women, and children alike got lost in the tomato and corn fields," my father would say. It was hard for me to understand how anyone could get lost in fields. I could walk for miles with Ignacio and his herd of goats and find my way home with my eyes closed.

I knew my father's asking me to help him in place of my mother was a very good opportunity to show him I could work alongside him just as my mother had. I was becoming a person with knowledge, but I could also show my humor. I believe I was ten years old when I knew the difference between the kernels of corn. They came in a variety of colors. What we would be planting today was for human consumption. Then I remembered humor might demonstrate to him I lacked seriousness toward the work before us.

My father would plow a rectangular form with one continuous furrow. The large field would be divided into two or three parts, and each would be plowed in the same fashion. The land was always plowed at right angles, to the direction in which rows of corn were to be planted, so the rows could be kept straight.

Tonta moved slowly, getting her hooves into the ground, and I took four kernels of corn out of the pouch that was swinging over my shoulders. I was able to drop the four kernel seeds in front of my left foot, but I could not move my right foot quickly enough to cover the seeds. I looked around me, and the field now appeared to be larger and wider than I had imagined. My father looked back, hoping as he made his turn at the end of the furrow, he would find me right behind him. What he saw was me lagging behind, throwing the four kernels into the ground, and using both hands to cover the seeds. "*Pendejo* [stupid], look behind you!" he screamed. The birds, the ugly ones, were picking the seeds from the ground.

When I saw my father walking toward a tree to break off a limb, I knew I should show no fear or cry out. If I did, the blows would be harder. So I closed my eyes as he hit me with the limb on every inch of my body. When he finally stopped, I saw the tree limb covered with blood. He had hit me with such a blow that there was a large, open wound that ran up and down my right thigh. Blood was running from it, and blood was now in my eyes. My father told me to go to the pond and wash off the blood so I could be presentable. As I limped toward the pond, he told me that for the next couple of days I could return to my mother's garden.

I returned to the shack smiling at my mother and hoping she would stay silent. I did not want to cry before her. A swarm of wasps followed her as she walked toward my father when he returned from the fields. I hated having such a thought, but I could only hope the wasps would deprive him of his senses, not kill him, but put him out of his compulsiveness to control everyone and everything around him.

Everyone shared in Father's blows except for my mother and Gertrudis. Alfonso was the most damaged. Neither Ignacio nor I could look at Alfonso when he was being given his share of the beatings. I do thank my father that he did not treat us differently.  We took our blows one by one.

Our mother did try. She would whisper into my father's ear, "You need strong sons to do the labor so you don't need to hire more workers to have more money to buy cattle and buy a home in town. You need to think more clearly." My father then said, "Someday they will thank me for making them men." He would take his hands in hers and thank her for his sons. In those moments Ignacio, Alfonso, and I knew we had a purpose. Nothing was accidental for our father.

She had her own share of scars even though he never hit her. I would think about the punctures and bruises on my mother, hidden underneath her worn dress. The work was brutal; she picked cotton, cut down and processed sugarcane, and tended to everything and everyone. What for? Ignacio, Alfonso I, and even Gertrudis would ask.  "Could she not go back to abuelo Juan?" "No!" She was not going to work like a mule on her father's land when she could sleep on hard ground that belonged to her. We were country people. My mother and father had no other thoughts but devouring every inch of dirt, and nothing was going to be wasted. If only this Virgin could take one seed and make it multiply into hundreds and drop them over the fertile fields being showered with rain, then she could follow with a clear blue sky and a rainbow. But even though I had a child's intelligence, I knew I could not have these delusions.

Maybe we were all delusional as long as we were inside the fence. Something inside my stomach wanted to be pushed upward, to throw out the thought that we were all delusional. My mother believed she could continue to forgive my father, my brothers believed they were more than just another pair of hands with two legs and a strong back, and I now was starting to believe that with my knowledge of numbers and the ability to read and write, I could pursue happiness. *But just look around you*, a voice said. What did it matter what I had learned in school? Nothing had changed on the farm. My father's idea was that I would be the man who would understand the value of a centavo for his precious farm. As he observed me, I knew if I had to be like him, I would be eternally agonized. That thought was too great to bear. I was nothing like my father, I told myself. I was too young to see, that in becoming a man, strange thoughts were being pushed deep into my brain. I was being consumed with shame, because I was not becoming the man I should be.

I did see my father laugh at times, especially around my younger brother Israel, named after our father. My brother did not seem out of the ordinary, other than that he was the dark one in the family, with coal black hair, dark brown eyes, and olive-colored skin. My intense jealousy started to recede when I saw my father giving my brother affection. I realized this man did have a place in him that was sentimental. There was hope for me, I thought.

He took out his own disappointments on his sons, and for me, the blows, while others were around, shamed me. I felt pressed down because I could not be the man he wanted me to become.

# Chapter 14

# The Sins of My Father

I fell ill for three weeks. I laid flat on my back on a bed, wrestling with what was truth or fantasy. It would have been easy to fall asleep and never wake up. What did I know about contaminated drinking water? In truth typhoid sooner or later appeared in someone's family, and it had befallen me. My mother brought me to a place. This place appeared unknown to me for I rarely visited my parent's home in the town. I could hear a voice in the distance. I could not tell if it was morning or night, dreaming of being in the wooden wagon pulled by our horse Bella with the milk cans clanking, and Bella not even moving an inch. When my surroundings became clear, I remembered I had entered school again and was given the responsibility of selling the milk in town since my father no longer trusted Alfonso.

Was it a dream? I could not smell the farm or my mother's scent, but I could see Alfonso wearing my father's tattered hat, and there were silver coins flowing out of his pocket. I could not push the thoughts of his great blunder back into the recesses of my mind. It was all too true though. He had been selling the milk from the goats and cows to his own customers and failing to tell my father. How could he be such a *pendejo*?

There we were, in my confused memory, my mother, my sister, Ignacio, and me waiting for one of them, my father or Alfonso, to make the first move. Maybe Alfonso could have lied about where he got the coins, but he did not. "I am not going to continue working like an animal for nothing!" Who would make the first move? "Run Alfonso," I wanted to scream, "and keep running!" Alfonso did not even move an inch.  My father lunged forward, put my brother into a headlock, and took him down to the ground. You could see Alfonso smiling while his face turned red. My father started to kick him with his knee into his ribs, and then he towered over him, took his foot and started to strike his head from all sides. Alfonso took every blow and did not cry out in pain.

Finally my mother took her oversized arms and pulled at my father as his energy was weakening. My mother reasoned with him; he was going to kill his son over milk.  What was left of this man, my father, as he walked back into the shack? My mother sank to her knees, and I could see her lips moving, "You cannot sleep with us in the shack Alfonso."

Alfonso pointed to his ears, and said he could hardly hear. What could a doctor do? Alfonso laughed. Soon it was dark outside again, and inside the shack, Alfonso was surrounded by bodies formed together in a circle. I was there with him gazing at the stars through the small hole in the ceiling.

81

82

# CHAPTER 15

# DID SHE BLEED?

I found my mother's hand. I wanted her to stop telling me when I grew up I would make something of myself, and she would be proud of me. I did not find it odd that I had no will to live. I was in the natural state of nothingness. What would be waiting for me tomorrow? I could hear the shuffling feet on the earthen ground. My body could sense their fear, and I wanted to take a machete and cut out what made them afraid.

It seemed like days between the times Gertrudis came to see me. I felt from her cold lips on my skin that she was experiencing a *susto* [fright], so far-reaching it was consuming her. It was not just my illness and possible death that was frightening Gertrudis. I heard the words pouring out of her mouth as she confessed something that was real to her and unbelievable to me: "Father has pushed himself into me. I think he has raped me." I understood what a rooster could do to a hen, but how could my father lose his senses? Gertrudis only shook her head back and forth, with tears rolling down her face, as she told my mother the story of the corruption, the straying of my father. I wanted to pull Gertrudis toward me to embrace her, but even though in my heart I was a boy, I knew I had to be a man. I had to show her respect for her virtue, and I was too weak to even cry for her.

In my delirium I was now dreaming of the rooster chasing my sister. I wanted her to run to the sugarcane fields; certain the rooster could not find her. But the rooster had cunning. Gertrudis was too simple to outsmart the rooster. Gertrudis' crying would turn into hysterical laughter; I knew she was close to losing her mind.

As soon as I regained energy and felt somewhat better, I saw things had gotten worse. My mother could not send Gertrudis back to the farm but not sending Gertrudis back would raise questions. Could she lie? Could she tell one story upon another story creating endless lies? Once the evil began, it took a life all its own. Abuelo Juan, hearing the accusation and knowing Gertrudis had no reason to lie, shouted that the sin was bringing shame to both houses. The profanity and the anger he felt filled the air with such heaviness it could have suffocated us all. Abuelo Juan believed Gertrudis and did not care what his brother-in-law Don Andres Guerra believed. His granddaughter had been violated. To make matters worse my father did not deny what he had done. What was my mother going to do? The Guerra family was telling her Gertrudis was a liar, insisting my mother's suffering was a trial to demonstrate her allegiance to the Benavides and Guerra houses.

When my mother and younger brother returned to the farm with me, we left Gertrudis with abuelo Juan and abuela Maria. I could see only that my poor sister's dreams were shattered. There would be no dances and delicate, ready-made dresses.  Even taking the veil would be out of her reach, some of the townspeople would say.

Because of my illness and the time my mother spent in finding a place for Gertrudis to detach herself from the past, I had missed many days of school; I would have to start school the following year. My mother believed that to protect her children's inheritance, she had to return to our farm. My father saw my mother's return as a sign of forgiveness, something only he could imagine. When he attempted to return to his habits of harsh discipline, my mother challenged him. She was discovering that my father's need to make men of us had confused his sensibilities.

To my father, my mother was just a woman; a backward woman he would never have anticipated would go to the authorities. But she did turn him into the authorities. Possibly she did this because he showed no remorse for what he had done. She would protect Gertrudis, knowing Gertrudis would be shunned by family and strangers alike.  He was arrested, tried, and sentenced in a court with the punishment of ten years in prison.

What happened to my sister had begun to define her because of the endless gossip. The wound was open for all to see, and the reporters coming from every direction wanted the lurid details. Of course, so many people could not believe that my father could violate his own daughter. "Still, why is he in prison? For nothing?" some would say. The townspeople and the reporters alike tried to pursue what they called the truth, but in reality the former enjoyed the gossip, and the latter wanted to sell newspapers. Theirs was not an honorable business, calling my father a despicable man, more animal than man.

The talk and the sensationalism created more disharmonies between the two houses. Abuelo Juan and my mother believed the Guerra house would spend any amount of money to destroy the Benavides family. If she would just say her daughter had lied, everything would return to what had been before, the Guerra families insisted.  My mother did what was close to her real nature, to protect her daughter's respectability and honor. The Benavideses stood by my mother and her children. Even abuela Maria, who was reserved and had more prayers than opinions, sided against her brother Don Andres Guerra.

Still my mother's anger, mixed with hopelessness, did not stop her from what she believed to be love for her husband. How could there be love? Abuelo Juan believed she had been hexed, but he knew there was not enough money to remove the spell of love. The Guerra family spent large sums of money to have the long sentence of ten years reduced. But during the year he served in prison, my mother sent his sons to visit him. I would open and read her love letters to him, and the love letters he sent back to her. I did not understand how she could demonstrate her need for him. I remembered her saying so many years ago to Gertrudis, "You will have to sleep by your husband's side regardless of any pain in your heart or mind." She had wed him for life. She only needed to remember some of the ballads she sang to me. Sometimes the pain is too great, and you have to leave the one you love. She was too consumed with the idea that with love anything can be conquered. What options did my mother have? Could she jump in the creek and float beyond the bend, leaving her children behind?

# CHAPTER 16

# FATHER BELIEVING IN THE BRUJELA

As if things were not bad enough, my father sent the *brujela* Hermelinda, her husband Juan, and her adopted daughter Esperanza to live with my mother. He had banished himself from the farm when he was released from prison. He went to live with his brother Romano, who also believed Gertrudis had made false accusations. So from afar he chose to court my mother, to seek her hand, and persuade her there was no need for a divorce; the separation was enough punishment.

The reason he sent for this *brujela* was not because he was non-religious, he believed in God, but everyone knew there were evil omens, invisible to the eye, that the *brujela* could cure or take away. This betrayal, the breaking of the two houses, would need potency to completely remove the stench and bring a restoration of the natural order of the farm. He knew my abuelo Juan would repeat, over and over again, "How can my daughter be so fooled?"

I would perch upon the highest branches of a tree and observe this *brujela*. Her skin was a chalky brown, and she had a short, stocky frame, and her coal black hair stood up on all sides. Her eyes spoke to you. With one look she wanted you to believe she was a weak woman. Then, when her eyes showed anger, you knew she wanted you to believe; she could destroy your entire being. She had looks that led you to believe you could lose the use of an arm or a leg or even your eyesight. Standing before the animals, open fields, crops, and the shack, she would chant daily "evil come out" and "come in good luck" and perform the sign of the cross over and over again. Her chants changed when animals started to die. She would tell my worried mother it was natural for animals to die to take the evil with them.

In the shack my father had built for the *brujela* and her family, there were snake skins, potions in glass bottles, bird feathers, and amulets. In the midst of all this was their sleeping quarters. I could only imagine Esperanza, her daughter, having nightmares, as she was surrounded by this world that most would never enter.

Even abuelo Juan started to believe real evil had entered the protected enclosed fence, and when he came to visit his daughter, he was concerned malignant spirits would attach themselves to him. But it seemed the *brujela's* spells might be working. It rained that summer, making the land rich.

The *brujela* started to be seduced by the land. She started to ask for payment, no longer with money, but with title to land. Of course, at first, my parents hesitated, especially my father, but then if he could offer what meant most to him, it was a higher possibility the effect of the spells would be granted. But it became obvious to me that something would need to happen, lightning to strike my parents, to bring my mother back to reality. Could my mother not at least see that all would be lost to this woman who had made a pathway into the fears and superstitions all-consuming to both of them?

My mother was not alone in believing in witchcraft. The entire countryside and even every town had pockets of believers. Abuela Maria would kneel alongside my mother, and together they would pray to the Virgin. Abuela would pray for my mother to return totally in heart and mind to the Virgin. My mother would pray that the Virgin would hear her mother's prayer. I sensed her shame in believing the Virgin had disappeared from her life.

# CHAPTER 17

# THE HUMMING STOPPED

Gertrudis knew instinctively she would have to leave before our father returned to the farm. She saw the packed bag with her personal belongings in the corner of the kitchen the day she had returned to the farm. She was not to speak to her brothers about the transgression. She was not allowed to go to town under any circumstances.

Our mother and her sisters, my aunts, were obsessed about finding a proper spouse for Gertrudis. It took them less than three months to convince Miguel Montemayor of the advantages of marrying into the Benavides clan. This had great value for those who understood pedigree. Gertrudis's beauty was undeniable, and she could sustain any hardship.

I wished Gertrudis happiness and embraced her for what I believed would be the last time. I could see in her dark eyes sadness even while she was smiling and telling me she was so happy to find such a handsome and good man like Miguel Montemayor. He would give her a new start in a different town with his family. She and my brothers knew that the Guerra house would always believe she had lied about our father. It seemed so wrong for her to be banished, never to return, while Father was waiting for the day after this, so he could plant his feet on the soil, the land that had claimed him.

To show his gratitude to his brother, who had given him refuge, he worked the land as if it was his own. He knew with Gertrudis's disappearing from the farm he had an opportunity to return. My father wanted to persuade my mother he was a changed man. He was very patient.

My father started to visit my mother each Sunday afternoon at the second meal.  They pretended the *brujela*, her husband, and her daughter were just guests, no better or worse, even as they walked the farm freely. The *brujela*, they reassured themselves, was somewhat normal; after all, did she not have an adopted beautiful daughter? I found this Esperanza enchanting, and I did not need any spell to feel my love for her. No chants or desperate wishes came out of her mouth. My father admired Hermelinda's husband, because he did not want any pity and would work as hard as the able-bodied laborers, even though he had a foot that dragged to his side.

We all asked searching questions. How this man could be married to such an ugly woman, with all her dreadful chants, and eyes that appeared to be a beam of dark light that could enter your soul? I wanted to tell my mother the *brujela* was willing to pay me to have sexual relations with her. She had asked, and I had refused. If I had told my mother, she would have told me to just avoid Hermelinda. I now had many responsibilities which had their natural rhythm. Hermelinda had no boundaries; I could believe she could fly and, that just by thinking bad thoughts, she could change man, woman, or child into an animal.

She lived with my parents for what seemed to be like an eternity. When she died many years later, I saw her husband, where at one time he dragged his leg he now stood upright on his two legs.

My father finally returned to the farm at the end of 1944, and now the people in town and the countryside said the farm could be called a ranch. Was this to make my father feel complete? Ignacio, Alfonso, and I asked our mother why he had to return.  Ignacio and Alfonso could see themselves becoming rightful owners of the land. Our mother reassured us that it now would be different. She would have more say over what happened to her sons. We should wait and see the transformation.

The Guerra family could not imagine my father returning to my mother, who had disgraced the Guerra house. The Benavides family could not believe she would open her heart to my father. The ties were broken, and we were shunned by the Guerra family. If you crossed paths in town, an aunt or uncle would walk past you looking directly at you with their teeth clenched. We had done nothing, but we would pay for our father's sin.

My mother no longer spoke of the past. Would there ever be a day when they did not have the *brujela's* name on their lips? Could the *brujela* bring a day when the world would forget the terrible transgression? She had promised, with the right amount of land given to her, anything was possible. Could you satisfy her quest or anyone's bottomless need for what belonged to others? I was too young to understand how envy can consume someone's senses.

My mother had done her best to manage the farm, but it was true, she needed my father. For sure, my father had not changed. His unhappiness had come about, he believed, as the result of his sons being given too much freedom. They were lazy. Even Ignacio, who was building a reputation as the best shepherd in the countryside, was losing invisible goats. At first my mother showed determination that the farm would not be run with my father throwing blows just because he believed it was the only way to turn boys into men. Fortunately for Alfonso, Ignacio, and me, we had been given time for our studies while he was gone. Our mother knew all her sons needed to read, write, and know their numbers. She knew all of us would have a future if we learned more than farming.

As soon as Alfonso heard that our father would be returning, he decided that working for my father would not change his circumstances. He knew he would not inherit any land, and he did not believe our father respected him. He needed his dignity. Alfonso would have to open the gate and walk to the other side alone. *Costumbres de mal maestro, sacan hijo siniestro* [a bad master's habits, make a sinister son]. He was not willing to be the sinister son. So he left.

I hoped he was choosing the right path, because he had his mother in him too. Our father was blind not to see Alfonso had also been seduced by the land but also wanted to dance and make his father a partner, not be a slave to his father. Alfonso wanted to walk alongside him. Alfonso had a natural gift for persuading others to see both sides of any issue. He could have been anything, but unlike me, he would react and then be regretful so many times. At least I learned from his adversities and his blunders.

The rhythm of the farm did not change after Alfonso left. Some things could not change regardless of how much power and money my father gave the *brujela*. My mother's memory of the words to the songs she had sung to me from my earliest recollection seemed to be gone. Shortly afterwards, the humming sounds she made as she went about her daily work went away too. I knew it was remorseful silence. Like other women, she took her fate and was thankful for any blessings, great or small.

95

# CHAPTER 18

# LEAVING THE RANCH

Alfonso returned to the farm after being gone for a month, but to me it seemed like a lifetime. My mother ran to the fence when she saw him. At first she scolded him for taking such a risk, but he entered with my mother knowing he could not have brought any evil with him. As she embraced him, she warned him that if his father saw him, he would beat him for leaving and then beat him the next day for returning.

It was pure luck that I was at the house, when I should have been feeding slop to the pigs. We were all waiting for my father to appear with the farm all over him. Alfonso put his long arm around my shoulders. He took American dollars out of his clean, white-cotton shirt pocket and rubbed them together. I knew at that moment I would rather work on other people's farms then be told every day that I was worthless. Worthless is how Alfonso had seen himself, but my mother and I knew differently, and perhaps he now knew too. He looked at me and asked me if I wanted to go north.

Why not? Why ride a horse when you can drive a car or get on a train to anywhere? Of course, I felt this was another sign my destiny was not too far away. I had overheard my abuelo Juan say that up north was a land of gold. You could save money, return, and buy land. Of course, I had to believe that because I knew my father had purchased this land with the money he had reaped while cutting down trees up north in Oregon, the land where water froze up in the sky.

What Alfonso needed was a man who had patience and was good with numbers.  He was deaf in one ear, but he could see I would provide him the ability to weigh the facts of any situation and come to a good decision, if only he would listen to me. I felt that, in time, what I lacked in strength I could make up in cleverness.

I had to think about what I was leaving behind. I would be leaving Bella. She had become my horse, and now I groomed her and fed her extra corn. We had something in common: we both enjoyed our freedom. When I would ride her out to pasture, we did not have concerns about the times she struggled to pull the wagon or my being reminded I might be kicked as a non-human. I had to always remind myself that my father was trying to make a man out of me. Some moments, his beliefs became my beliefs, but my true nature did not accept it. Right now Bella was strong, but in time she would no longer have any purpose and become expendable. We were all expendable, animal and human alike.

If I prayed for anyone other than my mother, I prayed for Bella. My prayers were short and to the point. "Please God, could she be fed and watered each day and given time to rest." When she died, I prayed she might be buried under a large tree, and possibly when her time came, my father would let her out of the corral so she could roam free on fertile grounds and die naturally, no one being angry that she could no longer do the hard labor her kind was born to do.

I knew my mother did not believe a young man, going on fourteen, would unlatch the fence to find freedom. Even though I was thin and lanky and could work twice as hard as most young men to keep up with my father, I was still a young boy in her mind. I could partly blame her since she put the dream in my head that I had a different destiny. She was not supposed to change her mind not at that moment. School was no longer on my mind. I was moving beyond the fence for adventures where I would no longer hear about *brujelas* and spells. I no longer would need to climb trees or get lost in the cornfield to avoid harsh punishment. I wanted to control my own destiny.

Finally morning came, and the first meal was served just like it had always been. The night before, my mother had given me new clothes a white cotton shirt, pants, and leather shoes. As she put pesos into my hand, she said, "This is enough for your return trip." What else would I need to walk out the gate, I asked myself.

My father walked into the shack and asked me if I thought I had become man enough to leave the ranch. I told him yes. My father nodded his head up and down. Then he laughed and told me I probably would not last more than two weeks before I returned with my tail between my legs. I knew my face was showing shame, turning red, like it always did when he wanted to humiliate me in front of those who loved me. Maybe my father really did not want me to leave. Now Ignacio and Israel and the hired laborers would be left to show their contentment with farm life. In my mind, I believed I was going on an adventure.

Up there in the north was the gold that could take a man from working on someone else's land to owning his own. I saw the money as allowing me to get established, by finishing my studies when I was tired of adventures. Someday, I would write like the reporters in the newspapers my mother had so closely hidden under the rock placed under her new bed. Why did she hide the paper? She was odd at times. There was so much I did not understand about her.

My mother embraced me, and I put one foot in the stirrup and then pulled myself onto Bella. Dust was kicked up by Bella's hooves, her hips swaying back and forth. There was that odor I would miss. For Bella and me this was our last trip together. I knew she would be taken back to the ranch by Ignacio who rode beside me. He wished me good luck and said that possibly he would head north someday. "It does not make sense to leave what you love the most, your goats," I told him. He was an excellent shepherd. It was a gift. Ignacio looked like abuelo Juan, and when he laughed you could believe that it was abuelo Juan. I knew for many years Ignacio would be the one who would surrender his life to my mother, always staying close to look out for her best interests.

I will always remember when I turned around; I could see my mother, father, and Israel standing there watching me leave. I saw my mother take one end of her worn, bloodstained apron up to her face to wipe her tears away and with her other hand she waved goodbye. I became intensely aware as the first drop of sweat started to roll down over my eyes that I was leaving her there with my father. He had fallen in love with what he did not have, a gentle soul. She saw something in him that was invisible to me. Possibly, I told myself, I will understand this when I become a mature man.

I knew she would continue with her daily routine, raising a family in harsh conditions, losing herself in being my father's possession. She had finally divorced my father after the incident with Gertrudis, to display to all those who cared, that the Benavides family again had their honor. They would not marry again. Yet she would always forgive him. My father, as he stood beside my mother, had only one thought: it was almost mid-morning; he had to return to the fields to work alongside the *peóns*.

I knew I would be the person to put the small headstone on my mother's grave. That was a dreadful thought. Why did my father put this in motion? The world for me was beginning to shift, and I no longer needed the memory of my sister Gertrudis's face, although she appeared in my dreams dancing in circles and jumping off cliffs. At first the dreams brought fear, but in time they brought me comfort. She was finding her happiness, and like our mother, she was looking forward and not to the past.

Alfonso was waiting for me at my aunt Felita's. We all said our goodbyes, and Alfonso and I were off to Reynosa, Tamaulipas. I could have been any age. I just knew I was now a man.

# CHAPTER 19

# CROSSING THE INVISIBLE BORDER

We met up with Alfonso's friend, Jesus Salinas, and his son. I paid the driver of the truck to take us to Reynosa where we planned to cross. The owner of the canoe, Marcos, said, "The Rio Bravo is shared with the people of the north. Everyone wants the water for themselves. People can be very greedy and unscrupulous and are always fighting nature." My father was not unscrupulous, but he could have been called greedy by those who had less, and definitely he was fighting nature believing profanities would kill the wild plants in his cornfields. Marcos said, "Water should not be just for watering crops; it is there for the good things – just for swimming," he laughed. I told him I could swim, and he laughed again and said that was a very good thing.

Stepping onto the other side of the Rio Bravo, I had a sense of real purpose.  Quickly reality set in when I started to feel hunger, something I had never felt before. Between us we had a dollar. The money my mother had given me had already been spent in getting us to Reynosa. In the days to come, I would learn that when you have money, you needed nourishment more than anything. Otherwise, the lack of it reduced you to no more than a famished, starving animal.

It is hard to explain, but I did not have anger toward my father for his lack of love for me. But I had not given up needing him to love me. I thought it was so natural to love him. I carried this thought that day, as I planted my feet in the north for the first time, and I would think this so often that it became a sickness.

But there was no returning to him as I stood on the top of the hill. It did not matter where the road would take me. I knew then there was no clear path before me. I would have to use what was innate, the ability to evaluate what I needed, in order to survive. I did not want to lack food or water. I needed to be clothed. I had new shoes which would keep my feet from harm. My destiny was before me. I had to repeat these things to myself over and over again. It was only an adventure. I looked forward to the next day.

## REACHING FOR THE GOLD

Looking out to the horizon, I could see the sun setting. It shined like gold. Alfonso asked, as we walked, if I wanted to return to the farm, where my father would tell all the farmhands that I, Ricardo, had no dignity. Alfonso was beginning to irritate me; he knew there was no turning back for either one of us.

With us were men, women, and children walking through the night. I did not know we were all going to Alamo, Texas. I would hear the mothers telling their children that they needed to look forward to picking vegetables and beautiful strawberries. No fear was reflected on the mothers' faces as they kissed amulets of the Virgin of Guadalupe and made the sign of the cross.

In time we decided to rest. There was no shelter, not even an old shack. A man, Jesus, with a wife and two children, invited us to sleep under a tree and to share tortillas and dried beef and water from a ceramic jug. We did not want to take from the little that they had, but to deny him would have shown disrespect. I could see trouble ahead for them. Having the least experience, I wanted to warn him that this venture was not meant for women and children. I kept these thoughts to myself though.

I wanted to take my fingers and touch the star my mother had pointed out so many years ago. She had to have believed one was just meant for her. She told each one of us that regardless of where we were, we could always see the stars above our heads. "Even the most half-witted person could see the stars," she would say. Each evening, we would look up at the same dark sky. I could pretend she was alongside me when I closed my eyes. Sharing this with Alfonso would only have given him one more thing to demonstrate to others that I was truly less than a man. My thoughts turned to the *brujela*, but I closed my mind to her.

It was hard to escape, to avoid Alfonso, as we trekked down the dirt road. He was a strong presence. Every morning he looked respectable regardless of whether his clothes were unkempt or not. His hair, bleached from the sun, had turned a golden blonde. People were enchanted by and admired his pale blue eyes, massive shoulders, and long strong arms out of proportion to his body. Alfonso could call a stranger an idiot or use profane language that abuelo Juan had taught him. He showed no fear when someone wanted to take a fist to his face. It did not matter to him. The harder he fell, the more alive he would feel. To me there was something wrong with this thinking, because if he injured an eye or had an arm broken, he could find himself on the fringes without food.

The long walk during the day away from the road continued until Jesus, his son, Alfonso, and I found a shaded tree where we could rest. We knew we had to find someone who would hire us; even if it was only one of us, we would share our good fortune. Alfonso, being resourceful, had found us water from an abandoned well, and we all sipped from a rusted can we discovered in a trash pile. Alfonso was able to look toward the horizon and see outlines of objects that would fulfill a human need. All I could see were outlines of rocks, prickly trees, dry dirt, and wild dogs. Alfonso and I never spoke about the *mal puestos* abuelo Juan had told us were outside the farm fences. It was as if the Rio Bravo had captured all the malignant spirits, sucking them all in, mixing them with the mud and casting them into an abyss. Abuelo Juan had never told me such a story, but I wish he had. I wanted to believe the *brujela puta's* evil hexes could never reach me.

I heard a rooster crow. Where you found a rooster you would find his hens clamoring and pecking the ground. The rooster reminded me of what I wanted to forget. He had his way with the hens; it was his nature. The hens instinctively never really tired of the rooster; it was embedded in their breeding. I wondered, just for a second, if I had inherited my father's characteristics, his marks you could not see with the naked eye. Would I inherit his compulsion to fix things?

Hopefully, the woman who owned the hens would have some work her husband refused to do. As we walked by the wood and stone house, a gringo came out on the porch, yelling "*Quieres trabajo* [want work]?" Alfonso put his hands on my shoulder and told me not to say anything. I heard Alfonso for the first time speak the words "We can be at your service, sir." The man replied, "For two weeks' work you will be fed one meal a day. You can sleep out in the back." His wife said, "There is water out back.  It tastes bad, but it is better than nothing."

The American wanted us to clear his land of wild plants and tumbleweeds, cut down dead limbs, and remove all the wild vines that were trying to choke his trees. We had work for two weeks. We were eager to use our muscles, to loosen the tension among our group that had built up since we left the other side. Jesus and his son, who rarely spoke, now bestowed gratitude on my brother. They were ready for his orders.

The man's wife gave Alfonso a large glass container to hold water, a package of flour tortillas, and a bag of rice and beans. There was a grill out back, and she handed us tin plates, an iron skillet, and a tin pan. Each of us was given a spoon. It became very important to not let any food fall from the plate. We smelled bad, but there was nowhere to bathe, so we found ourselves washing our faces and hands and underarms with the foul water.

We ate in silence. I could remember the three meals and the hot cocoa my mother prepared each day on the farm and being surrounded by those who all looked through the small hole of the ceiling, where at times I imagined the *Indios* chased the Spaniards around the moon.

As I lay on the ground looking up at the stars, I questioned if this was the adventure I had in my dreams. In dreams, I did not need food or water. Would I become a wanderer like the crazy woman who passed through the farm and was told repeatedly to stay off the property by my father? From where did this crazy woman come? Was she lost, or did she believe she was on an adventure? No one seemed to be concerned that she was all alone, talking to herself and barely dressed. She had to belong to someone.

After two weeks, the man gave Alfonso what looked to be eight pesos. I was expecting my share, as now I was working alongside my brother. Alfonso told me that for now he would take care of the money. He gave Jesus and his son their share.

# CHAPTER 20

# THIS IS OUR LAND?

Evening came and we jumped into the back of the truck with other men who were also heading to Alamo. There was excitement. I found myself smiling at the men who said there was work for everyone. Still, I was uncomfortable with so many strangers surrounding me. What evil did they bring with them? There were no longer fences as there had been at the farm. The thought disappeared as quickly as it came.

We were to go to Gregoria Guerra's home. Even though she was blind and a widow, she did very well for herself and her six children. She had supported her children by taking boarders to stay in the largest room of her small house. She embraced us, making us feel so welcome that it was easy to forget we were only distantly related, somewhere in the Guerra clan. Her son was working in the orange groves. He told us he would approach the patron tomorrow to see if he would hire his honorable relatives and friends. Her son was well respected as we found when we went to the orchard the next day.

The work at the orchard was not difficult for Alfonso or me. We stayed together pulling oranges off the same tree. He stood at the top of the ladder; I picked closer to the ground. If I fell behind, he would come behind me and throw the oranges in my sack. I had to keep pace or lose the job to those who were less connected; there was never a shortage of able men.

After working in the orchard for hours, everyone would head to the showers.  When I saw most of the men with muscles from the strain of picking day after day carrying heavy sacks over their shoulders, I was not embarrassed; because I knew what I lacked in strength was made up in cleverness. One evening while I was in the shower, an old man, who appeared to be alone and too old to be working in the orchard, handed me a bar of soap. When I was ready to return the soap, the old man was gone. Alfonso and I agreed to share the soap, and pay the old man for his generosity, but I never saw him again.

The day I sent my mother my first letter was the happiest day since I had left the other side of the Rio Grande. My letters were always the same: I was working every day, learning English, loved her, and knew she could never be replaced in my life. Her return letters were always the same: she was staying strong, Ignacio and Israel missed me, and she loved me so much. I should never stop writing, and she looked forward to seeing me again. There was no mention of my father.

It was best for Alfonso to ignore the men who slept beside us, knowing Alfonso would easily spit in a face and with a clenched jaw prepare for the first punch. Alfonso enjoyed the tension and the reaction. He enjoyed giving and receiving. For me it made no common sense. How could he not understand the unpredictably of the consequences?

I watched every evening as Roberto, one of the pickers, lowered his eyebrows and squinted his dark brown eyes. He spoke louder and louder about how the Spaniards raped the Indio women. "Those Spaniards would rather marry their own cousins to keep their blood pure and the riches close," he would say.  "Look at Ricardo hiding in the corner; he has no clue that the ancestors' blood in his veins has been tainted, corrupted with selfishness and greed," said Roberto. He then asked what I thought about a raped woman. I was not going to share the secret of what my father had done to my sister. Women were to be pure. No one wanted a whore.

Surrounded by these men, I now learned we all had something in common: we were illegals. It was illegal to enter the north without papers. But if it was so illegal, how could there be a field of Mexicans picking oranges? To cut the trees in Oregon, my father had to have broken the law, and this was totally out of character. I wanted to understand how so many Mexicans could be working the harvest if it was illegal. The old and young alike would laugh. "The orange trees rest on top of lands that used to belong to Mexico," they would say, "so in a way we all are toiling over our own land."

But senseless dreaming does not provide you nourishment. I knew these men could not deny the fact that in Mexico land was owned by a few. My fellow countrymen had no choice but to endure adversity. The strength in their bodies had to be matched with determination in their minds and cohesion of the idea that they were a consequence of a history not of their choosing. They were *campesinos* [country people], people of great minds, not just *campesinos* who picked for the farmer.

NO
DOGS
NEGROS
MEXICANS
20 FEB.1929
ALAMO, TEXAS

# CHAPTER 21

# NO TROUBLEMAKERS

I learned that having light skin could be your friend or your enemy. Alfonso and I would walk into a restaurant where over the threshold above the door was a sign, "No colored or Mexicans." My blue eyes, sandy blonde hair, and blistered sunburn could fool others who looked like me. Roberto, who was of the darkest shade of brown, considered me his enemy, but he held his animosity when I handed him food. At those moments, I knew Roberto would have traded places with me. It was not a figment of my imagination that I was able to relieve myself in an inside toilet when the others had to relieve themselves behind bushes and trees. In those moments, I knew skin color did matter to others. I was not favored by God though. There was nothing to be gained by distinguishing between the races; all it did was breed resentment and hate.

As long as Alfonso had his walk with Conchita, Mrs. Guerra's daughter, in the evenings, he was happy, and laughed at Roberto and any of the other men. He had courage. Without his courage, we would still be walking the road, experiencing the pangs of hunger.

The orchards provided shade from the blistering sun, and the clean surroundings in the showers were a true luxury. The men spoke of following the harvest, but they did not look forward to picking tomatoes in the fields. It was an opportunity to work alongside wives and children, but the women aged too quickly. You could go all the way north to Michigan, where the sun still burnt the back of your necks, but you would find comfort from the many cloudy days there.

The owners would come to the orchards in their trucks and walk up and down the orchard and laugh. The patron was well respected by the owner, but at times he would bow his head and say "Yes sir," and "No sir," just like the *peóns* who worked for my father. The owners did not want any troublemakers in the orchards; there was a system there and a need for harmony to keep the system in place. There was no place for those who habitually caused trouble. The troublemakers would be uprooted and be escorted off the property, courteously or by force.

It was a sad day when all the oranges were gone. The memories of my first shower and all those to follow at that orchard would carry me through the days and sometimes weeks when I could not bathe.

# CHAPTER 22

# HE KNEW

It became blatantly clear that my father knew about the road Alfonso and I were walking. He could have tied me to a tree on his land, but he had not. He could have explained to me that it was illegal to cross the border. He could have explained that I would be hungry, and that the color of my skin could be my enemy or my friend. I believed I was clever, but the Americans, the gringos, wanted my two hands and had no interest in my ability to use numbers. It was no longer an adventure. I had to think quickly; I feared my father more than anything. I became thankful that he had not told me of the perils. I had thoughts each day would be a better day. What my body could endure was easier, than how confused my mind would become by returning to him.

Alfonso and I disagreed on how we were going to divide the money I had earned. I understood his reasoning. He felt he had made the contacts to earn money with a tolerable place to sleep each night. It was true; I did not go without anything.  I could argue that I worked just as hard, took care of him when he drank too much tequila, and only complained about my clothes and lack of good shoes. He laughed at me. "Who do you think you are?" he asked.  I could hardly believe my own ears when I answered, "We are both sons of our father!"

Many of the men and their families decided to head farther

north. Alfonso and I had other plans; we would stay together and look for another farm in Alamo to see if we could clear their land or whatever we could find.

*La migra*, what Americans called immigration officers, finally appeared one day as we walked down a dirt road, searching for someone to employ us. We were put in a car and thrown on the other side of the border. We found ourselves back in Reynosa. We had four dollars in our pocket, and we would take the bus to General Trevino.

Hearing that we were in General Trevino, our mother made arrangements to meet us in the plaza. There had been some changes in her. She could not keep her soft blue eyes open. She was physically with us, but she was weak in spirit. She was becoming detached from our world. I wanted to tell her how youthful she looked, even though I hated to tell a lie. I feared for my mother as she spoke about how many spells she needed to learn. She just could not keep them straight in her mind. We both pleaded with her to leave the farm and return to Abuelo Juan. She needed to return to the Catholic Church, Alfonso told her. She reassured us that she prayed to the Virgin, and the *brujela* no longer had a hold over the farm. She knew the worst was behind her.

119

# Chapter 23

# Indoor Plumbing

When we left General Trevino again, Ignacio came with us. Now our mother was left with our father, our brother Israel, the hired workers, and the brujela and her family. As we rode the bus to Reynosa, under his breath Ignacio said over and over again, "Virgen, cast out the wicked."

Again, we found someone to take us across Rio Bravo, but this time there were no thoughts about swimming in the cool water. My thoughts were on how to avoid la migra. We walked through the entire evening and then rested under a tree. Ignacio carried a bag over his shoulder filled with dry beef, oranges, and a canteen full of water. We hoped we all could get work in Alamo. Alfonso found work in a processing plant, but Ignacio and I could only find sporadic work. We stayed in Alamo for a few months, before we found ourselves with no money to buy food. We slept on the ground looking up at the stars or finding relief under a tree from the blistering sun.

We left for Raymondville, Texas, where many had heard there were onions to pick. We walked a great distance from the dirt roads, sometimes with others, conversing about having no clouds in the sky to shade us from the sun, and how we all welcomed rain. We laughed at ourselves for believing that up the road a farmer could provide us shelter with indoor plumbing and a private bathroom. Regardless of what the farmers thought, we cared about cleanliness. We could hear the men, "They pay fifteen or twenty cents a bushel, which would be sufficient to buy food and some type of liquid." Our pangs of hunger and thirst were tempered by our high spirits.

Ignacio and I did not speak about what we had left behind. We did not speak about his goats that would be put out to pasture by a stranger or about my desire for an education to fulfill the destiny my mother spoke of throughout all the years. On those evenings with only a pencil, I would write my letter to my mother, not on a piece of paper, but on the ground. Ignacio did not laugh at me. He understood how I felt inside.  We both missed her.

We walked and walked and then rested under trees, and then we slept on the ground. It was a relief to feel the wetness on my face from the drops of dew the next morning.

We came to the onion fields. Some of those who had walked with us were turned away, but Ignacio and I found ourselves picking onions. I was not accustomed to the onions, so tears started to flow. I began to cry, not just from the wretched onions, but at how empty life appeared to me now. Feeling empty did not remove the need to drink milky, brown warm water from a bottle strapped to my pants to quench my thirst. The water in the glass bottle was worth more than gold. I laughed because there was not any gold. It was a great myth this land of gold.

After four or five days, we began working in a covered building sorting the onions by size. Some of the campesinos were envious of those who had familiarity with the owners of the farm. We understood the importance of not complaining. Being submissive kept you employed and causing trouble disrupted the workers around you. There were stories about Raymondville, where you might find yourself incarcerated, never to be seen again for violating the laws. Those surrounding us hoped the missing ended up on the other side of the Rio Bravo.

We had found an inexpensive place to sleep each evening.  I cannot remember the woman's name, but she bought me clothes to wear since the others were torn and frayed, and I was to pay her after I received my wages from the farmer. This was the first time I saw men cursing the farmers for treating them like animals. I laughed when one man said in his drunken stupor, "A queen, a farmer's daughter, would be so appropriate to reign over Raymondville. She could become queen of the onion fields!" One after another the men spoke of the spectacular procession and ceremony throughout Mexico for Our Lady of Guadalupe. Nevertheless, all the men agreed that Our Lady of Guadalupe loved the farmers and their daughters.

## JUST A HARD BACK AND STRONG LEGS

I had never seen a procession or a ceremony for the Virgin. There were many things I had not seen in my own country. I was ignorant of so many things. Ignacio just smiled, and I felt empty. I missed those evenings when Abuelo Juan told us stories to give us a reprieve from our challenging circumstances. I was learning so much about Mexicans. There were Mexicans who were American citizens. So why were they called Mexican? There were no obvious differences between the Mexicans who were born on the northern soil and all the others. Some of them spoke English, but Spanish was as close to their character as it was to mine.

One day la migra removed Ignacio and me from the farm. We knew someone had to have called la migra, possibly the farmer. Possibly, it was another campesino who had believed us to be unworthy of sorting the onions. As we walked by the farmer, there were no dollar bills in his hands. We were now left with a few pennies in our pockets, no longer even in possession of our few belongings. The poor woman who had provided us with food and shelter was a casualty of the affliction, her reward for taking in strangers. What we had left behind had no real value, other than my pencil. She would be lucky to sell it for a penny.

We rode to the border with men, women, and children, whom we knew would wait till dusk, and then go back north to the fields where they would find another farmer's bounty to pick. His bounty ensured there would be money to pay for their basic needs. Some with families could save enough to send money back to their relatives on the other side of the border.

Hunger can make you a thief, but we knew there were always

the garbage dumps. You could gather cardboard or beat-up steel wires and whatever else could be sold in town. My bare feet had to be protected as we walked through what the rich had left behind. The shoes my mother had bought me, I had lost somewhere, and it did not matter because they no longer fit. My obsession of protecting my feet would be tempered, when I could find cloth to wrap around my feet and ankles. One nail, causing a limp, could be a missed opportunity to be hired at the next farm. You always had to worry about harming a limb, a hand, feet, eyes. However, you could always work if you were deaf.

I had realized the majority of these people around us had no choice but to follow the harvest. I could have stayed on the farm and worked for my father, but I could not bear his abuses or the townspeople and my flesh and blood of the Guerra family looking directly into my eyes with contempt because of the scandal. I knew the brujela, with her grotesque behavior, was still on the farm, influencing my mother, who was completely losing her reasoning.

If I could have chosen between Alfonso and Ignacio to walk this long road, it would have been Alfonso. Alfonso spoke about women loving men. "Just with our blue eyes, we could mesmerize any woman," he said.  Where I lacked charm, he could teach me to be mysterious. Women were attracted to men who had secrets and concealed their true character. I had no secrets, nor did I understand what character was. Were character and temperament one and the same? Alfonso spoke about white Americans having their pursuit of happiness. They were, at times, confused and threatened when colored men wanted what was true to their nature of opportunity and freedom, to sit side by side with a white man. There were poor people everywhere, but sometimes they could not see their similarities because of the color of the others' skin. Alfonso was so insightful at times, and he enjoyed feeling life to the fullest. But sometimes, it seemed like he had a death wish.

When Ignacio and I had hunger pains, I would think of our Virgin Lady of Guadalupe, who all men and women spoke about in the fields, in the kitchens, and while the women hung the clothes on the rope lines. Who was this lady?  My mother and Abuela Maria prayed to her. How could she charm so many people, even those working in the fields where mothers would weep for their children? Would the Virgin watch over the children in the bountiful fields? I realized that as much as I wanted my father's love, he had given me something possibly more important. I was taught to read, write, and do my numbers. Never mind if the intention of educating me had been for his personal use. I was finding that many did not have these practical gifts.

Putting one foot in front of another and looking down at our bare feet, Ignacio and I spoke of our days playing in the creek and of Teresa. Her own dream meant she really only wanted to express herself as an individual. She did not want to become just a mother, as I did not want to become just a farmer. It was better to speak of Teresa than our need for nourishment. Ignacio, Alfonso, and I no longer needed to wonder what was past the bend in the creek that we had spoken of and drifted to, during what seemed many years before. There had to be more than what we had found on the roads we had traveled, and in the fields we had toiled under the sun. Why were the Mexican people just two hands and a back to the farmers? The people who worked the fields conducted themselves with integrity. Yes, there were a few who could be ridiculed for being too slow, by getting lost in the idea that this was their destiny and their children's.

# CHAPTER 24

# DO NOT GET DISCOURAGED

One day as we looked up at the horizon, we believed there was a large sack in the middle of the road, forgotten. This was good luck, we told one another, as Ignacio put the forty-pound bag of flour over his shoulder. We began laughing as the skin on our lips started to tear. Not much further we saw smoke rising from the side of the road. There was an old woman, with the most fashionable and beautiful scarf, preparing tacos on a mesquite wood fire. We did not care why this woman was alone, even though it was odd. We traded the flour for tacos and a few pesos, so now our stomachs were full, and we could claim we were not penniless. As we went on our way, we looked back, and we could no longer see the old woman. Could this have been another coincidence, like the old man at the orchard who gave me the bar of soap and who had never been seen again?  Possibly, this was some sort of sign for me to not get discouraged, to move forward, to rise above my circumstances.

That evening we slept on the side of the road. It was pitch black, the stars so bright and belonging to no one but me. I told myself, if I were a rich man, I would buy the stars and the inhabitants. I would want to protect them. They did not need to see how one can have so much and the other so much less. I did not want their hearts to be broken. Ignacio did not have to say anything. We could read one another's mind. We missed our mother, and we were afraid for her. Her oldest sons and daughter were gone. We knew her mind was drifting, but she had more strength than most women. If anyone could overcome the spells of the *brujela*, it would be her. My mother was too virtuous to be swallowed up by the likes of Hermelinda.

The next day, we found ourselves in Reynosa as la migra found great pleasure in removing us from the land that had once belonged to us. We jumped on a train with others like us hitching a ride to Los Herreras, Mexico. The conductor was a kind man.  He took one look at us and knew we lacked money but, to him, we seemed very trustworthy. Our luck continued as we were taken in a taxi to General Trevino, Mexico by a cousin who was a stranger to us. In General Trevino, I found myself alone. Ignacio had returned to the ranch to work alongside my father. It was not so much that he was seduced by the land as he just wanted to be a shepherd. He would die a shepherd at the age of eighty-two. He worried that he had not accomplished very much in his life. The only inheritance he could give was his goats. I reassured him that what he left behind was worth more than gold. He had never coveted what belonged to others, and he had always been joyful for other people's blessings. He truly had treated others as he would have wanted to be treated.

In General Trevino, I was greeted by my sister Gertrudis and my brother-in-law at their door. There standing between them was their daughter, Graciela. They shared their home with me. One evening her husband put his arms around Gertrudis and Graciela, and they danced to the rhythm of music we could hear, but I was too embarrassed to ask why people played such music for all to hear. I sensed melancholy just below the surface, but with her husband full of love and devotion, I kept it concealed.

I wanted to follow Ignacio to visit my mother, but I was afraid to see my father.  The rejection of his much-needed embrace would be too hard for me to bear. Then, too, I reminded them of the past they both were trying to forget. My mother sent word she was sending money. I should go to Monterrey and attend school. I was to take the bus, and in Monterrey I was to ask for Gregoria Reina. Everyone knew of her. At the bus station in Monterrey, I found myself surrounded by strangers. I was now confident at the age of fifteen. It did not matter if my clothes were worn, and I lacked a pair of shoes.  I pushed the words out of my mouth, "I am looking for Gregoria Reina."  People shook their heads, but in the midst of the confusion, Pedro Salinas introduced himself to me.  He was a student at the university, and he actually was staying with Mrs. Reina. Such good fortune, I told myself.

130

## CHAPTER 25

# WHO IS FIGHTING PROGRESS?

Mrs. Reina's home was not an orphanage for wayward individuals who could live freely under her roof. I gave her the money she requested, and I began attending school during the day wearing new clothes and shoes which I had purchased. Pedro helped me with my studies in the evening. At school I was surrounded by people who knew nothing about following the harvest. I always remembered my mother telling me not to speak about the farm, but did she expect me not to speak of the illegal workers in the north? I was being taught about a Mexico where all individuals had freedom, and told we were not to fight progress. Possibly they were speaking of the depraved *Indios*?  Or were they speaking about those who go north to follow the harvest? I had chosen to cross the Rio Bravo and not return to the farm. I had made my choice. What about the hundreds of others, who had no land to really call their own, and lacked the sophistication to mask their lack of education or connections with no chance of improving their station in life? What would the future and "progress" hold for them?

In time I wanted to stand on my desk and yell "Viva Mexico!" I started to believe that only progress could raise up all Mexicans from poverty and injustice. It became explicit, the curtain was raised, and all I could see was the progress of every single person to have access to an education. It was a purist idea. I did not want to think about how many men, women, and children toiled under the unforgiving weather. Even for the short time I picked onions, I believed my back would break. I did not think I could take another step. I did not want to remember those I left behind in the fields.

Two months passed, and then just as fast as my good luck had come, it was taken away from me. My mother could no longer pay for the cost associated with my education or my room and board with Mrs. Reina.

I found refuge with my mother's sister, Maria de Jesus, sleeping in her kitchen, while I paid her with wages collected from my job as a waiter in a restaurant. Pedro became my good friend, which was a great surprise, since he was a refined gentleman and I was a farmer's son and a fruit and vegetable picker. He told me often that I had so much potential, and I should continue with my studies. Unfortunately, that was impossible, since I worked ten-hour days, and on Sundays I picked fruit and anything else I could get my hands on. Now I had to focus my thoughts on progress beyond the wages that barely gave me any real freedom. Now when I thought about destiny, and foolish ideas, I would just whistle out loud to drown out the thought.

133

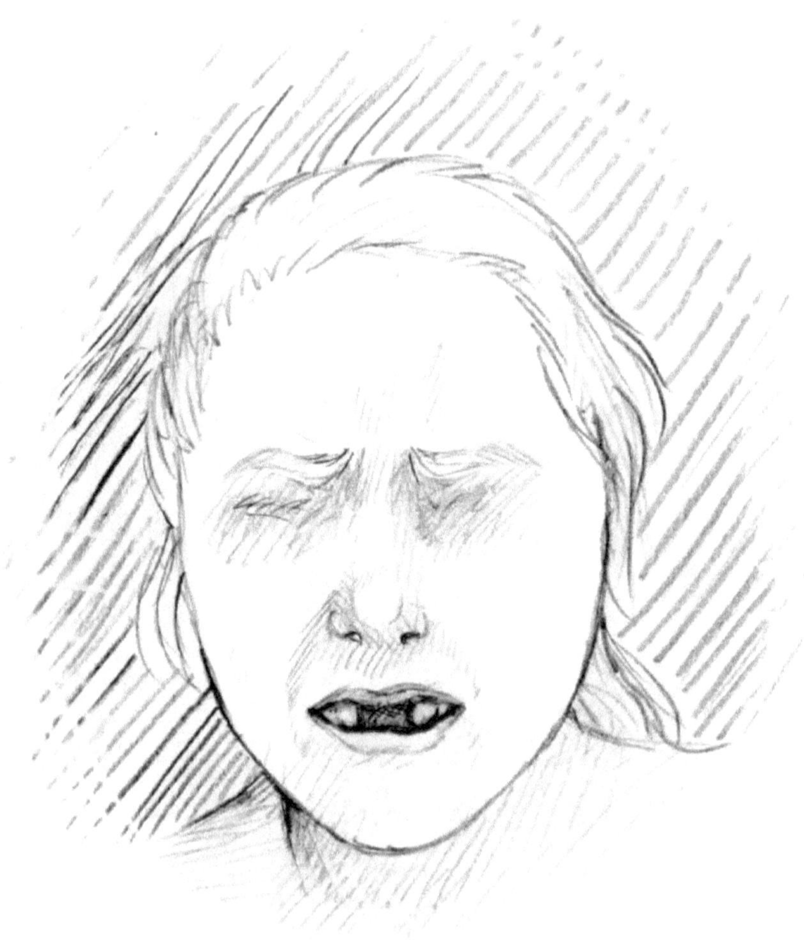

# CHAPTER 26

# THE SHUNNING

In October, 1946, I was notified by my aunt that my mother was having problems and needed to see a doctor. The owner of the restaurant agreed not to replace me for the duration of my mother's illness so I could go to see her.

As I traveled on the bus to town, my thoughts were going in circles. They had not said it was a broken bone or typhoid or even a blow to the head from a fall. All I could see in my aunt's eyes was anger when she told me.

Entering the back courtyard, I found abuelo Juan and abuela Maria with their eyes fixated on my mother, who was chanting words into a piece of picked cotton gripped in her right hand. As she came towards me, her eyes flickered. She recognized me, but I could see her eyes close as she started to chant again, this time wanting to "cure" me. What was I to think? I knew by looking at my mother's eyes she had been overtaken by fear; she had been suckling witchcraft. Where was my father? Abuelo Juan answered that he had done this to her; he was the crazy one, the weak one, the one who would leave his mark on all his children. Abuela Maria took my hand, "There are no prayers to take away what your mother now has," she told me sadly.

So, off we went, Mother and me in a taxi. She was mumbling to herself, and tears were streaming down the face I had kept in my memories. These memories comforted me when I believed I was not loved. I wanted to remind her that Ramon was buried somewhere alongside the road so many years ago. But in her state of mind, I realized she might believe she needed to raise him from the dead. When I arrived at my aunt's, she refused to let her sister in the door. She reminded my mother how she had divided the family when she accepted my father into her life again. "She has had to endure so much, and now you want to turn her away as if she was a leper," I said.  I wanted to ignore the tears cascading down my face. I wanted to contain my feeling of hopelessness.

My uncle, a compassionate man, could see that my mother needed to be protected from what he could not see, and he pushed the door wide open. My aunt came to her senses. We all knew that measures needed to be taken to release my mother from what appeared to be a frightful dream.

The specialist doctor came there with his equipment. The operation seemed to go so quickly. I saw him put an object in her mouth, so she could not bite her tongue, and put wires on her head. I believe she was given a shot. I was not afraid for her. They started the treatment, and she jerked. I knew in a modern world there were things I did not understand. It was over, and my mother slept for hours. When she awoke, her mind had cleared. She asked me, "Why are we at my sister's?" I could see her eyes had softened, and she had returned to us. I explained an incredible procedure had been performed; she had been given shock treatment. I described the remarkable skills of the doctor. She thanked the doctor, but I could see shame in her eyes. What I saw was a miracle, the miracle of medicine, but she saw herself as a weak woman who had disappointed so many.  Now she had brought more shame on the Benavides house.

That evening I overheard my aunt saying that no one would open their door to her except abuelo Juan, but what kind of life would that be? She knew my mother was not a mad woman, but everyone in town would believe she had been touched by the devil. The townspeople would take no responsibility for her condition. The shunning, the gossip, and the blaming of her for what happened to her daughter would drive anyone to break from reality. Israel Guerra's body being dragged in town behind the aggressive muscular stallion would be a proper way for him to die. How could my aunt wish this?

I told myself firmly, there were no devils, and there was no hell. The next morning I found my mother gasping for air. Her mouth had turned bright red. Beside her was an empty can of some type of acid. She had tried to take her life by pouring acid down her throat, but it had not been enough. The Red Cross took my mother to the police station, where she had to give a statement about why she was trying to kill herself. She shouted, "Can't you see I want to die?  You all think I am crazy and a lunatic, but I am not. Do not take me to the hospital."

Of course, in the hospital, they fed her through her veins. So for a month, I stayed with my mother at the hospital, believing modern medicine could cure anything. After a month passed, the doctors told me there was nothing that could be done, and it was better for us to return her to her family. She would die, as her body was shutting down due to the lack of nourishment, and her spirit was becoming weaker. The shock to the brain had brought her back to reality, and the *brujela* no longer had a hold on her. But the pain of everyone knowing of the treatment would make her live in the margins, in the shadows, until her death.

No matter what, she was a child of God. This did bring her comfort. She accepted her fate with resignation. We did all we could by spoon-feeding her, but I could see in her eyes that she welcomed death two months later.

# CHAPTER 27

# FACE THE WORLD I SAID BUT IT WAS UNTRUE

What will I have left of me to be remembered?" she asked me. "Your children are your legacy," I said.  I shared with her how Ignacio, the shepherd, had paid for all her treatment and had sought the right stone to put on her grave. We spoke of Gertrudis's daughter, Graciela, being so curious about the world and her good spirit.

I spoke of how parts of her spirit were left in each one of us to face the world with confidence and soundness. Alfonso was industrious, congenial, and so forgiving of others. Israel was still a young man and found the ranch comforting, and someday he would own the ranch. For me, I found comfort in being a private man, observing others, but most of all, never tiring of her telling me of her love for me.

My father had been looking for atonement because of what happened in the past.  My mother was relieved when she knew that the brujela and her family had moved off the ranch. My father's atonement could not be found with a spell which he finally discovered. My mother cried so deeply when she would speak of my father. He would have his land and would marry again. The idea of someone holding him close and sharing his dreams only meant her release from this world could not come soon enough.

How did I want to remember my mother? She was the essence of pure love. She made my existence tolerable. She gave me parts of herself, the restlessness, the need to find answers to my endless questions. She was an amazing woman, surrounded by people and living in a period where she was demonized for protecting her family, even when her dignity was taken from her. Her circumstance did not define her. She showed me that a woman could be as brave as a man.

My father wanted to see my mother before she died, but abuelo Juan had only one thought, and that was to drive my father, his land, and the evil brujela to the burning abyss. Her death came as she was surrounded by those who loved her.  I placed the stone on her grave. None of my abuela Maria's Guerra family, my father's side of the family, came. They probably believed the lie would be buried with my mother.

"This is my story as I remember it," and her father laughed as he wiped his red nose with his handkerchief, the same frayed handkerchief he had held to her face when she cried because of childish disappointments.

We will not be returning to the father land, the small town in Mexico. My holding onto that dream kept us from moving forward. We were all stuck in time.

"Would we be stuck in time if Mexico had won the war against the United States of America?" he asked. There would be many answers to this question. For many men like her father they dreamed of possibilities.

141

# ISABEL DELIA GONZALEZ

Award Winning Author Isabel Delia Gonzalez had a business career with a Fortune 500 company spanning over twenty-years. During this tenure her hallmark was the ability to frame critical issues into messages that resonate with and move audiences to action. The importance of corporate citizenship Gonzalez involved in non-profit Board service, concentrating on the global community in building bridges between diverse cultures is vital to bring peace, love and harmony to the world.

As an author, Gonzalez has earned major honors from the **International Latino Book Awards** for her two books, *Breaking and Bleeding a Macho Man*, in 2017, and *El querbrar y sangrar de un hombre macho*, in 2019. The International Latino Book Awards is one of the five largest book awards in the USA and the largest diverse book awards in the world.

Her experiences in International business provided access to international business executives and consulates from the global community, including but not limited in coordinating high profile events with China, Germany, Spain, Mexico, Brazil, and Venezuela.

Her knowledge in marketing, publication relations and diverse technology applications provided success in building relationships between the corporation and non-USA Governments.

As advocated over thirty-year period for second-language requirement for all students beginning in primary to university level in the United States of America. In addition to embrace students who have a native language other than English to retain the native language and learn English to facilitate full participation not only in the United States of America but globally.

Gonzalez formed Scribbler Company to advocate on behalf of those labeled mentally ill. Because of the lack of empathy and indifference the three largest mental health providers in the United States of America; Cook County in Illinois, Los Angeles County and Rikers Island in New York. This indifference has developed the need to understand not only this is a global human rights issues but also a civil rights issue.

Gonzalez is an Empowering Speaker on the important topics of Mental Health, Women Studies, and Children Education.

*"Because of the lack of empathy by many politicians worldwide the mental health system is disjointed if there are any services at all. With the lack of empathy today the three largest mental health providers in the United States of America: Cook County in Illinois, Los Angeles County and Rikers Island in New York."*

# BREAKING & BLEEDING OF A MACHO MAN

Mexico born writer, Isabel Delia Gonzalez fictional book based on her observation of men believing machismo is the badge of courage. They have been conditioned to believe the courage is more important than life itself. What are the consequences of the conditioning?

This story is as timely today as it was 200 years ago. Story of tragedy and success will be told by an old man to his daughter.

The old man's story beginning in 1928 is set against the backdrop of a waning Mexican revolution and a mother telling her young boy his destiny is not to be a farmer as was his family before him, but a man of knowledge. Was her belief in his destiny tied to the color of his unusual white skin? The inner conflict of this man's story arises, from the strength of the unconditional love from his mother, and the destructive forces from his father.

Continually surrounded by superstitions and cultural conditioning of the Mexican machismo, the son can only see people becoming monsters, the bastardization of religion, the influence of witchcraft, the horrors of incest, subjugated women with no dreams, and the falsehoods of the "modernization" of Mexico.

What were the consequences to this old man of his emotional solitary confinement to protect himself from the forces of his surroundings trying to take his sanity away? Was his distorted inner world real? What did the outer world see in him?

Adhering to his distortion all those who touched him are pulled into his machismo world.